Aphrodite's Sister

The Angel

Kelly Balch
Book II

Table of Contents

Chapter 1

A day had passed since I'd said goodbye to Montana. My first year at an all-mortal college had come to a close, and summer break was beginning. I stared down the street to where my house was—on Earth.

My chest felt heavy, so I sat on the curb and waited for it to subside. I didn't want to think, but my mind would not obey. My home in the Heavens was no longer open to me. The law forbade me. I was officially in exile, and I felt like an outlaw. How had my life changed so suddenly?

It had all happened much too fast for me to give forethought to the horrible consequences—or to consider that there would be any. I was Petra Ambrosi, the Goddess of Emotion. The Olympian Elders had given me my gift, which was the ability to feel every being's emotion while my own heart remained stone. In the Gods' eyes, it was a great gift, but to me, it was a curse.

However, everything changed for me last semester. Something happened. I felt an awakening in my chest. My emotions started to evolve and take over my body, not allowing me to think or control what I was feeling. And all this began with a kiss from Taylor "Montana" Letto.

If Taylor Letto was not the mortal goddess of the sweetest lips, then she was the Goddess of Destruction, for her lips carried with them the most brutal of sacrifices—I was not allowed to see my family. I had to wait until the Moirai, the three Goddesses of Fate, determined my fate and discussed it with Zeus, the father of all immortals. They would then decide upon my freedom or my banishment to Tartarus forever.

Tartarus was a hollow mountain of pain and suffering, the hell of all hells to which the Gods sent those who were the most evil and treacherous. And I could be considered one of them because of one ridiculous, amazing, earth-shattering kiss. That kiss had guided my fate toward those the Gods called Lambdas, the Enlightened—a hidden brotherhood among us. The Lambdas followed no rules. They loved whom they loved and lived how they wanted. If the Moirai decided I was a Lambda, I would be forced to join the Titans and all the other banished ancestors in Tartarus to suffer for eternity.

I felt my chest grow heavy once again, thinking about what was to come at home in the Heavens. My father Diomedes' leg had been healed completely, and he had returned to his seat at the council table with the other Elders and heroes of the past. My mom would be gardening with Demeter's descendant Laura, yet another great cultivation that would yield a bountiful harvest. I would miss seeing the look on her face when she first spotted the bounty. I would also miss bidding farewell to my brother, John, and sister, Eva, as they prepared for their training at Titanus school for Gods and Goddesses.

However, even if I had not been banished from my home, they would have hardly even known I was there anyway. In fact, it was the perfect time. They wouldn't even notice what had happened to me down on Earth.

So, ultimately, Earth was my holding cell until the Moirai handed down my judgment. In the meantime—as Nick Herms, descendent of Hermes, the Messenger God—had advised me, I had to try to forget not only Taylor's kiss, but Taylor herself. Forever.

I stood from the curb on which I was sitting and began moving slowly toward my house again, dragging my feet with each step, plodding reluctantly forward. When I finally reached the chipped, cream-colored door, I sighed loudly and pushed it open.

My mind was suddenly transported back in time.

I remembered the first day of school last year, in a classroom. Taylor stood over my desk. Her words were slow as she asked me to try out for the soccer team. Then I noticed something I never would have noticed if not for the delay. I watched the sweat forming on her forehead, and I heard her heart patter faster with each gulp she took. She was nervous. But so were two others.

I felt them sitting behind me in the classroom—Nick Herms and Jaden Krowe. I could feel everything they were feeling in the delayed-motion moment. They watched me, on edge and nervous. If Taylor hadn't been distracting me in that moment, there was a great chance I would have felt their emotions at the time. I was grateful to the Gods for giving me this recollection.

Nick and Jaden had been there. They had always been there, watching me, even before I knew who they were—but it felt like they had always known who I was. I could hear Nick drumming his fingers against his desk, as if waiting for something. What had disturbed his spirit? As for Jaden, why did she stare at me with such tenacity?

4

My mind woke up and flitted back to the present, back on Earth.

"What are you doing here?" Jaden shouted. She had a big smile on her face as she popped into the hallway. I smiled back at her, thankful I was not alone. "Did you forget something? I thought you'd left to go back home. Is everything okay?"

Her questions bombarded me, each one firing from her lips and piercing my skin like bullets. I tried moving past them—and her—toward the couch, feeling the need to sit down again.

After taking a few deep breaths, I was able to look up at her. She sat across from me with a wild smile on her face. I tried smiling back, but the reality of everything that had happened pulled like anchors at the corners of my mouth. I couldn't even fake one.

"What's wrong, Brosi?"

Was I that easy to read?

"Nothing." I was still a horrible liar. Who was I even trying to fool? "I'll be staying here for the summer," I muttered.

"Really?" she screamed as she hopped up from the couch. "That's great! I have a summer job, so I'll be staying here, too! We'll be together the whole summer!" She grinned at this conclusion.

"Yeah. Do you know of any jobs I can apply for?"

"No, sorry," she answered sincerely, not catching my sarcasm.

However, maybe it wasn't such a bad idea. It was the summer season, and I couldn't just wait around like a sitting duck for my trial. My mind would wander and make suppositions, making matters worse than they already were. I needed a distraction. From that and from Taylor. A job would be just the thing.

"Are you hungry?" Jaden asked.

I looked away from my pallid hands to her smile, a smile that could illuminate the darkest sea.

∞

When we walked into Sunflower Market, I immediately spotted the collection of red wine. I glared at the bottles as if they were friends who'd become foes. In my mind's eye, I saw Taylor struggling to extract a cork, pouring wine until our blue cups were full, and then pouring again until both bottles were empty.

I saw us lying in her bed—our lips touching, my hands running through her hair, our legs tangling as she pushed her body against mine.

I walked by the malicious bottles, eyeing them accusingly as I continued down the aisle—the same aisle I had desperately chased Taylor down, begging her not to buy them. Things would be different if I'd succeeded. I turned the corner, forcing the memories to the back of my mind, but as if a blow from Ares' sword had struck me, more began to play. The smell of the cinnamon bread she loved, the way she wore her sweatshirt hood to the side of her neck. Suddenly I wasn't hungry anymore, and I desperately wanted to leave the market.

"So what do you want to get?" Jaden asked, catching me off guard.

"Nothing." I paused, allowing her to stare at me, which she did, searching for something.

She released the stare with a pleasant smile. "Well, okay," she said and then turned and left my side.

I didn't know what was happening to me. It was as though Taylor had laid an egg inside my mind, and now that egg was hatched, freeing all the memories we'd shared. I couldn't stand being in the market any longer. I was already losing focus. I had to erase her memories and forget her.

I ran outside, back into the summer air, and the heat immediately thawed my skin with warming kisses. In front of the store, I sat on an eroded, wrought iron bench with weathering white paint. I began fidgeting with my nails, biting them as if they had done me wrong, all the while eyeing the mortals passing by. A sweet elderly couple walked cautiously across the street to their car holding their grandchild close to them. A group of young teenagers skateboarded across the parking lot, using the speed bumps as jumps. Then I spotted a small group of Regis students heading to the market in front of me. I wondered if any of them were deities. They might even be Lambdas who had also been banished and were awaiting trial.

I jumped up from the bench, excited by what my new presumption might mean. I quickly tried to figure out how to approach them. *What do I say? How do I ask them?*

Before another question formed, a sense filtered through my blood. I could feel her not far from me. She felt fervent, nervous.

"Ashton Janus," I whispered to myself as I turned toward where I was sensing her.

6

She had one hand in her pocket and leaned casually against a cart. In her other hand, she held a scrunched-up yellow T-shirt. Her smile grew so big her blue eyes nearly disappeared.

"Petra Ambrosi, what are you doing here?" She started walking toward me. Each step rippled with her emotions, like sound waves to my ears.

"Shopping," I answered dumbly.

"I know that." I was fixated on her mouth as she kept grinning. "What are you doing in town? I thought you'd be leaving."

"I'm staying here to find a summer job."

"To find one, huh?" She smiled. "Any luck?"

She sounded skeptical, and her interest felt fake. She didn't believe for one second that I was here just to find a job.

I gave her a condescending smile and sat back down on the bench. She followed me and sat down, scooting to the edge, and then turned to face me. I kept my gaze on the parking lot, trying not to look at her. Her stare did not let up.

"Not yet," I finally answered.

Her smile dropped. "You need a job?" she asked without missing a beat, which caught my attention. "I can get you a job."

I watched her carefully, trying to sense her thoughts. The last time I'd seen Ashton, she was standing near Taylor at Tawny and Sade's graduation. And she'd looked at me as if I did not belong. Now she was trying to help me find a job. She was just as confusing as Taylor. Yet, I could sense that she really wanted this.

"Come, we'll get you one right now."

She quickly stood and started walking through the parking lot. I watched as she took each step with the confidence of a predator after an impressive kill. She turned around and smiled at me, nodding her head for me to follow. I put my finger up, telling her to wait a moment, and ran back into the market.

Jaden was near the detestable wine bottles. I called to her. She grabbed one of them and walked over to me, cautiously, as if she were in trouble.

"Yes?" she asked, just as cautiously.

"I think I'm going to go get a job right now."

"Oh! Well, good luck!" She raised the wine bottle. "We'll celebrate when you get back!"

I left the market and saw Ashton leaning against a car no one should even be touching. I walked past the front, letting my fingers run across its sleek surface, feeling what my eyes had never seen before.

In the Heavens, cars did not exist, for the simple reason that there was no need for them. Throughout my time on Earth, I had learned the huge differences between cars and how they were distributed differently to each social class. This car was obviously intended for the rich—the very rich. The assumption quickly popped out of my mind like the embossed Bugatti written in chrome on the tail.

"Is this yours?" I asked attentively.

She flicked her head around to look at me, sending her hair cascading across her face. Her smile was her only answer before getting into the car.

Who is she and where does she come from? The thought jumped into my head and lingered there the entire drive.

We pulled into a parking spot outside the Coors Life Center at Regis University, and the car automatically shut off. By the time I slowly got out, she was already waiting for me at the front entrance. As soon as I entered the Center, every muscle in my body relaxed. My head drooped lethargically as I tried to zero in on where these emotions were coming from. My eyes finally focused on a beautiful woman at a desk in the back of the room. She smiled, and a glow unlike any other surrounded her. She was extremely happy to see Ashton, and it seemed like they were longtime friends.

I eyed the woman, intrigued. She appeared to be in her early forties, tall and slender, with the most beautiful caramel-colored skin. Her light brown hair parted on one side and curled delicately under her chin. She had golden eyes that glowed, and those eyes spotted me instantly. She began to speak in a tongue I barely recognized—the tongue of our great ancestors, from centuries before my time. No one used it anymore, only the great Elders when they talked amongst themselves. Or so I had heard.

Ashton turned around quickly and met my gaze, and it occurred to me that she had understood the woman. Her face morphed into a smile as bright as the one the woman wore.

"This is Petra Ambrosi." Her smile grew bigger. "She's my friend, and she needs a job."

They both kept smiling at me, watching me carefully, as if I were going to perform a trick.

"Is that right? Well, do you have any work history?" the woman asked, now in my own tongue. Her voice was alluring as silk.

I shook my head.

"Well, that's okay. What can you do? What are your skills?"

My eyes shifted to Ashton for some help with the question, and as if she could read my mind, she answered, "She plays soccer here at Regis—"

"She looks like you," the woman said in her seductive voice, catching us both off guard.

I looked at Ashton and tried to see the similarities, and she looked at me, searching for the same.

"What?"

"You two look alike. You could be sisters. Aside from her blonde and your dark hair, Ashton, you guys are practically identical." The woman walked toward me with an elegant grace. She stopped two feet in front of me. Her eyes wandered over me, crawling up and down before finally stopping at my eyes. Then she stuck out her hand. "You're hired."

I slowly reached for her hand, preparing myself for whatever emotion I was going to feel from her. I slid my fingers into her palm, and immediately my body dove in. I could not let go, nor did I have any desire to. I felt her breathing as though I were doing it for her. My eyelids closed, but I could see everything. I was in ecstasy. Everything felt perfect and blissful. I was at ease—and then I was suddenly awakened.

A burst of light shot out and sucked me into an endless darkness, and then I began a long fall. I landed near a river, a dark river. The air smelled foul. I was not alone.

I tugged my hand from hers and looked up at her golden eyes, now glowing even brighter than before. She gave a tiny smirk before turning around and walking back to her desk.

For the life of me, I could not figure out what had just happened. She was something ... not of Earth. She couldn't be a Nymphet or a Goddess from my generation. She was something more powerful. A Titanide? My brain would not seem to focus, but I felt certain I was right.

At Gaianus—the school for the demigods, or so I liked to call it—we'd learned that after the Titanomachy, the war between the Olympians and the Titans, Zeus had not banished the Titanides to Tartarus like many of their fellow Titans. I tried hard to remember the reason for this, and then it came to me. The Titanides were neutral—some even supported the Olympians during the Titanomachy. The ones who had not been banished could still be found in the Heavens, living with the Elders, but I had never seen any among the young Gods and Goddesses, especially down on Earth.

"You'll start work immediately. Get her a shirt, Ashton, and take her to the field house. She's all yours now," the Titanide said, smiling.

I looked at her, astounded.

She nodded at me before Ashton pushed me out the door.

I gasped. Ashton noticed and smiled at me.

How does she know a Titanide? Is she one, too?

I had to ask. It was now or never. "What are you?" I let it out in a whisper.

Ashton stopped walking and turned around. She was looking down at her feet, but I could see her grinning, making me wait forever for her answer. In a blink, she was standing in front of me. Without saying a word, she started to remove her shirt.

"Ashton?" I looked around to see if anyone was watching. "There's no need—"

She laughed and then turned around. My head was spinning, and then my eyes fell on the brand. The same Lambda brand Dion displayed on his forearm, and Allison on her wrist, was on Ashton's right shoulder blade.

"You're a Lambda? You've been a Lambda this whole time?"

She turned back around to face me and shot me a cocky smile before putting her shirt back on. "I have." She laughed. "I also knew you were a Goddess the whole time."

"W-What? How?"

"I just knew. You can tell." She shrugged.

"B-But... Wow." I gasped and shook my head. "Are you a Titanide as well?"

She started to say something, but then stopped and smiled mischievously. "What makes you think that?"

"You understood the old language."

She shook her head. "I dated Allison Prome. That's how I know their language." She looked at me as if I knew what that meant, and then gawked when she realized I did not. "Allison Prome..." She paused. "Prometheus. The Titan of

Intelligence and Wittiness. The one who stole fire from the Heavens and gave it to the mortals."

I stared at her blankly. I had become so ignorant that I had not recognized the similarity between Allison's surname name and that of her ancestor.

"That's how I know your new boss." She winked and started walking back to the parking lot.

"She's very powerful," I gasped.

She laughed and then turned to me. "Yeah, she is. You've just met Theia, the all-seeing, all-knowing Earth Titanide. Congratulations."

I was shocked and maybe a bit star-struck, as if I had met Zeus himself. A great and famous Titanide still living in my era? And on Earth? Was this a more common occurrence than I'd thought?

"So, is Allison considered a Titanide since her ancestor was?"

Ashton continued toward her car, not answering my question. We both opened the doors and slid into the seats. I waited for a handful of seconds until I could feel her about to answer, but then she hesitated, searching for words.

"There are many Titanides living among you, my dear."

Her answer was not what I had expected.

She reached for my hand and slid her fingers into mine, locking them tightly. I could feel what she wanted as her eyes met mine. "Let's not talk about her."

There was a long pause. My eyes focused on her lips again. Though her eyes were just as beautiful, my eyes expressed a different interest, lingering on her lips more than they should have.

"I'm glad you decided to stay here this summer," she said softly.

I felt her clearly then, through her touch. I continued staring at her lips, her feelings becoming louder with every passing second, until finally, without even knowing, she unveiled everything. She thought I had stayed on Earth for her. She thought I wanted her. I pulled my hand away hastily and stared out the window.

When we arrived at the Regis field house where I would start my new job, I stepped out of the car and began walking toward the entrance. Ashton was a couple of steps behind, keeping a great distance as though she was thinking about something. I entered alone.

Inside was a pool about forty feet long and twenty feet wide. I turned to face Ashton and saw her leaning against the door, smiling as if she had come to a happy conclusion from her previous thoughts.

"So?" I asked.

She pushed off the door and started walking toward me in that appealing way of hers, still grinning. She drew up beside me but didn't look at me, her eyes still on the pool.

"You'll be lifeguarding here." She smiled and then handed me a white shirt that read *'Lifeguard'* in cheap lettering. "You start now."

As she said it, a group of elementary-aged kids came running through the door with two counselors following close behind. I watched each kid leap into the pool with jovial excitement.

"What are you going to be doing?"

She smiled. "Supervising." She then nodded her head.

I looked at her, confused.

"Your post?" she said, smiling. "You need to go up to your post now."

I felt her enjoying herself already.

I climbed up carefully and looked down from the chair at all the kids in the pool. I could still feel her watching me, so I returned her smile and gave her a slow, dramatic wave. She hesitated for a second but then gradually made up her mind to leave.

Before she could go, I asked, "So what kind of Goddess are you?"

She stopped and pivoted slowly to face me, still wearing that grin on her face. She hesitated for a moment, shaking her head. "I was wondering the exact same thing about you."

Then she pivoted back around and walked out the door.

I stared after her for longer than I realized, not paying attention to the kids in the pool. They seemed totally irrelevant to my new train of thought: *Exactly who is Ashton Janus?*

∞

That first day at the pool I worked six hours. My duties included nothing special—just sitting and watching. I concluded that my job was completely pointless. Hardly anyone came to the pool, and if they did, it was usually a group of kids with more than one counselor looking after them. But I sat anyway, and I tried to look at my time alone by the pool as a kindness from the Gods rather than an annoyance. I was grateful I had a job to keep my mind off Taylor. Surprisingly, my mind denied thoughts of her very well, but it grew heavy with thoughts of my expulsion and wondering if I would ever see my home, family, and friends again.

Although I was not anywhere near ready for it, I prayed that my trial would happen soon. The thought of never seeing my family again was tragic. Would they really send me to Tartarus? That single question, ignited fear within me, a fire I had just recently started feeling. I shook my head to erase the thought and my feelings.

"Why am I feeling emotions?" I yelled out, thankful the building was completely empty. What was happening to me? "I am Petra Ambrosi, the Goddess of Emotion. I do not feel my emotions. That is what my gift is, isn't it?" I whispered. "Please Gods, answer me!"

Only one tear answered back. I looked at the skin on my hands—skin that no longer glowed, skin that had begun to feel pitifully mortal.

"Praying, are we, Petra?"

My head shot up to see Nick Herms across the pool. I narrowed my eyes at him. This was all his doing.

"I need to talk to you." My voice boomed through the hollow building.

"I know," he said gently. "That's why I'm here."

I hopped down from my post to meet him. He found a lounge chair to relax on, and I hastily sat on the one next to him and crossed my arms.

"Okay. Speak," I demanded.

"I see you've found yourself a job already."

I was in no mood for his banter. "How long will it be until my trial?"

He sat up and leaned toward me, placing his elbows on his knees, now understanding that I meant business.

"There's no arranged time. The Moirai will meet when it is time for you to meet."

"Will it take all summer?"

"Maybe. Maybe not." He shrugged slowly.

My next question was prefaced by a heavy sigh and came out sounding more hopeless than I wanted. "How do I fix this?"

He looked at me with sorrow, a look I saw so often and hated.

"Remember, Petra, I'm only the messenger," he said softly. "You have caught yourself in a web; it cannot be easily undone," he added in a hopeless tone similar to my own. "I warned you." I felt his tears although there was no sign of him shedding any yet. He fixed his eyes on me. "This girl, what makes her so special?"

I recoiled from his question. "Taylor? She's my friend!" My voice was grating and harsh over his fragile one. It shocked him.

"And you kiss all your friends?" he said, with a ghost of a smirk.

"No." I sulked.

A tear began to fall as Nick's sad expression come alive again. His heart was larger than he perceived it to be. As my own hot tears fell, I felt his heart begin to spin in an agonizing whirlwind. He could not hide his reaction from me, and that fact made me cry even more.

"What's happening to me, Nick?" I cried, giving in to the tears. I hated asking aloud, for it validated that there was indeed something wrong with me.

He pulled me into his chest and held me there for a long moment. As I heard the beats of his anguished heart, my anger began to soften. I embraced his pity and allowed him to hold me. It was something I had never done with anyone. I felt completely vulnerable for the first time in my life, and Nick Herms was the one to console me. Was this a God I could trust? Then, the vision of him sitting behind me in the classroom the first day of school came back to me.

"You were there," I mumbled. "Why were you there?"

"Where?" he asked gently, rubbing my back.

"You were sitting in the back of the classroom, next to Jaden."

His hand stopped rubbing, and his whole body stiffened. Abruptly, he released me, and I sat back up to look at him. His eyes were dark. I sensed something unusual from him that made me pull away even farther.

"Nick?" I asked again. "What were you doing there?" My tone was low and even, but I could not hide my apprehension. He saw the fear in my face and quickly directed his eyes away from mine.

"I was watching you." He seemed disturbed by his own answer.

"Why?"

"I was given orders to do so."

Fear traveled to every nerve ending in my body. Someone had ordered Nick to watch me. I could think of only three that would order such a thing.

"The Moirai," I whispered.

He said nothing. He didn't even look at me. His whole body was still.

14

"Why? I hadn't engaged in any Lambda activity then." I felt more tears trying to force their way out from behind my eyelids, but I used all my strength to hold them back and waited for his answer.

He remained silent for a while, before finally lifting his head to stare directly into my eyes. "Petra, I know this may be difficult to understand now, but trust me, all will be unveiled when the time is correct."

His emotions felt sad, but he sounded certain. With a stern look, he nodded to me to determine whether I understood. I could see in his eyes that there was so much more that I did not know. And although those green eyes hid his secrets well, I felt in time that they would be unveiled.

So with no more tears, I wiped my face and nodded my head.

∞

I walked through the front door and slumped down on the couch. My face was swollen from all the tears. I didn't understand why they'd fallen, and that bothered me more than the hidden secrets Nick's eyes held. I had no idea if he was someone I could trust. His feelings had spoken louder at the pool than ever before. They were forgiving, kind, and full of torment. I took pity on him just as he did me when he held me. It was a new side of Nick Herms, a new side that I liked.

I felt Jaden's excitement down the hall. I was way too tired for it, but had been expecting it.

"Petra!" She ran into the living room and jumped on the cushion next to me. "How was it? Did you get a job? You were gone a long time."

"Yes. I'm a lifeguard at school. I started today."

She jumped up from the couch. "Congratulations!" She made her way toward the kitchen and opened the fridge. "We should celebrate!"

She took out a wine bottle, ran to the cupboard, and extracted two glasses. I felt so low in comparison to Jaden's exuberant high. I had nothing to celebrate. I was an exile on Earth, a possible Lambda, my family was more distant than ever, and I had no one to talk to—not Apria, not Dion, and definitely not Taylor.

Although Dion was a Lambda, I felt I could not confide in him. I imagined that the high honor and respect he had always had for me would disintegrate once he heard the news. With that thought, I suddenly felt it again—fear. I waded in that feeling for a bit longer this time, trying to dig at what I was fearful of. Then it hit me like an overwhelming wave. I was ultimately fearful of what my family and friends would think of me. Would they still love me once they found out I had broken Zeus' law and become a Lambda? Would they disown me?

"I'm so happy you decided to stay here this summer!" Jaden yelled over the counter, her excitement pulling me away from my dreadful plummet.

I smiled bitterly. I hated hearing that word—*decided*. I had not *decided* anything. I would have never chosen this fate, just as I would not have chosen my gift.

Jaden was fiddling with the wine bottle opener as if she didn't know how to use one. A flash of her and Nick sitting behind me at their desks shot through my head once again.

"I'm glad I won't be alone," I replied as I rose from the couch and moved toward the kitchen in order to sense her better.

"Exactly," she said. "I thought I was going to be alone all summer. Diane went back to. . ." she hesitated, "back home."

Her concern and worry clouded the room. She had almost let her secret slip. She looked up at me and gave me a fake grin, and I smiled back.

Should I wait for the truth or go along with her secret?

"Where is home for Diane?" I finally asked.

She gulped nervously, her fingers still fidgeting with the opener. Just then, her hand slipped from the bottle, and we both watched in slow motion as it spun and knocked over our two glasses. All three hit the floor, shattering in all different directions.

Drops of a dark red liquid began to drip over the shattered pieces on the floor. I looked up at Jaden. The broken glass had managed to snag her hand before falling. She looked at me, horrified, as she held her hand tightly against her body. I could not stop staring at the blood spilling down her wrist and onto the floor.

Neither one of us moved or made a sound—only our breathing. She was nervous and shocked. My eyes remained fixed on her hand.

Just as I began to doubt my conclusion that she was really a Nymphet, her skin slowly began to heal itself. It was as if the cutting of the skin went in reverse—the blood quickly dried and the skin began to close until not a scratch, not even a scab appeared on her. We both watched the brand-new skin fully heal and then glow brilliantly. Jaden's head immediately shot up at me.

"Petra, I-I—"

16

"Don't," I said, laughing at her attempt.

"Petra, it's not what it seems," she tried to explain. I waited. "I'm… I'm—"

"Busted?" I asked.

"You weren't supposed to find out like this," she huffed, and began pacing back and forth, muttering, "Poseidon's going to kill me."

"What?"

She stopped pacing and looked up at me, confused.

"What was what?"

"Poseidon," I said.

"No." She shook her head. "I didn't say that. I didn't say anything. I ju-just stopped talking."

"Jaden!" I laughed. I grabbed one of the broken pieces of glass and dragged the sharp edge across my palm until blood spilled.

"Petra," she gasped, "you don't—"

Although it took longer than usual, my skin slowly began to heal itself. Jaden stopped pacing at once.

"See," I said, smiling, "I'm like you."

There was a shy grin on the side of her mouth. "I know, Petra." She sighed. "I've known."

My smile slowly began to fade. Suddenly it didn't seem like a coincidence that she was here. Or that she had been watching me in the classroom.

Did the Moirai send her here, too?

"You have?" I asked.

She nodded slowly. "Yes," she said, exasperated. "I know quite a lot about you."

"You do?" Now I began pacing. *Will I have to explain everything to her? Apologize and tell her the kiss with Taylor was an accident? Lie and say it was a huge mistake?* I began to pray to the Gods for their forgiveness.

"Yes. You are Petra, the Goddess of Emotion," she said. "You are the daughter of Diomedes, King of ancient Argos. One of your kin is John, descendant of Eros, the God of Love. And he attempted to end his fate." She paused for a bit and grinned. "That's why I'm here."

I stopped pacing and sat silent, confused. She wasn't here because of what I had done. She was here because of what John had done?

"You weren't sent here by the Moirai?"

"What?" she asked, shocked. "N-no." She squinted at me. "Poseidon sent me. He gave me orders to guard you. I'm your guardian, Petra." She said the last bit with a high-pitched cheerfulness that nearly made me roll my eyes.

I sat still as an iceberg. Was she telling the truth? Did Poseidon really send her, or was it the Moirai? I was afraid to trust her, afraid to tell her anything.

"We were there at Point Dume," she continued. "Me, Poseidon…" she paused, "Diane… and other nymphets. We were waiting in the sea for him."

We have a law in the Heavens, one of Zeus' laws, that as immortals, we cannot die naturally, as humans do. Only under extraordinary circumstances can we die. And those circumstances are determined by the Moirai, the Sisters of Fate. To the deranged few, immortality was a curse. They wanted their lives to end. Our alternatives to death were either banishment to Tartarus or going to the Elder Olympian Gods—Zeus, Hades, and Poseidon—and pleading for the pain to end. Only an insane, broken God would do this.

I had heard of mortals wanting to end their lives in order to find peace. However, for us, going to the Elders or Tartarus would never bring peace. Therefore, suicide attempts were extremely rare. Yet we'd had two in the past fifty years. And those two deities were my sister, Eva, and my brother, John. I shook my head at the thought and grabbed my forehead.

"He wanted Poseidon to end his pain," I whispered.

"But Poseidon didn't want that," she said as she cleaned up the glass and blood on the floor. "It was not your brother's fate to go just yet. John has much to do. Poseidon was seconds away from ordering us to stop him, but then we saw you." She stopped her cleaning and looked up at me.

I envisioned John on the cliff and started to feel his waves of torment once again.

"You saved him." She smiled. "However, Poseidon did not trust that he wouldn't try again. As we both know, Poseidon was right, because not too long after, John went to the Underworld to ask Hades. And there you were, Petra—the analgesia—saving him yet again.

"After his second attempt, Poseidon realized you weren't going to be able to save him every time. Especially when your mother had enrolled you in school here on Earth. So he ordered a few Nymphets to oversee him, a couple to watch your family, and me to look over you. And that, Petra, is the reason I am here." She let out a deep sigh of relief.

18

"Not because you have a summer job?" I asked.

She laughed nervously.

"You knew I was a Goddess," I mumbled, feeling the need to verbalize it in order to understand.

She smiled and nodded.

"You knew I was going to come to this mortal school?"

She nodded again.

"Is that why you were with Nick in the classroom?"

She hesitated, and then nodded slowly.

"My guardian?" I questioned.

"I'm here to protect you," she said again.

"From?" I asked. "Why does Poseidon think I need protection?"

She did not answer, merely pursed her lips and furrowed her brow.

"And why did he want you to keep it a secret?"

She shook her head nervously. "I only do what I am told."

That seemed to be the trend nowadays. Nick had told me the same thing just hours earlier. I held back from asking if she knew I'd been banished from the Heavens. My head felt heavy. Had she known this was going to happen to me? I didn't say another word, for I didn't wish to humiliate myself any more than I already had.

"Well, now that's settled…" She opened up the refrigerator, reached in, and pulled out another bottle. "Wine?" she asked, still smiling. Her green eyes were glowing brighter than usual. I nodded and then returned to my former position on the couch.

Chapter 2

The Crew

My guardian. Jaden's words echoed in my head—and so did the questions. What danger could I possibly be in to need a guardian? Did my family know they had Poseidon's Nymphets guarding them? There were pieces missing from this puzzle.

A little boy was looking up at me from the water below my lifeguard post. I had to blink a couple of times to focus on him, and I wondered how long I had been on my runaway train of thought, staring at him as if I were not alive.

It was my second day of work, and it was just as boring as the first. There were more kids, though, and every so often, one would do something so outrageous that I couldn't help but be amused. Seeing all the camp counselors in their bathing suits, lying out as if attempting to get a tan in the fluorescent lights beside the indoor pool, was humorous as well. No ray of sun could penetrate the metal ceiling.

I heard the door to the pool area open and felt a handful of people walk in, reeking with confidence. I didn't turn my head to them because the little boy still held my attention. He jumped out of the pool as I watched and felt him, walked over to a female counselor reclining on a pool chair, reached under the chair, and lifted it up high over his head while she was still on it. It looked as if she was floating. The little boy held her up so easily with one arm. I blinked rapidly in order to clear my head and decide if what I was seeing was real. I had nearly forgotten I was on Earth. Not long after, another counselor rushed over and picked up the boy, carrying him out the back entrance. I looked around at the kids in the pool, at the other counselors, but they all just went about their business. Apparently, no one else had seen the boy lift a weight three times his size over his head as if he were a descendent of Hercules.

Then I felt the group of people again, the cocky ones. I knew their stares were directed at me without even copping a peripheral peek. Each surveyed me with their different interpretations.

There were four of them—two females and two males. I spotted the blue-eyed man instantly only because he bore a striking resemblance to the Athlete God I'd seen paraded around Via Olympia during the Ten-Day Celebration. Just this past winter, he'd looked to be a boy, not the fully grown man with muscles standing in front of me now. His beauty rendered me speechless. I stared at him while they all stared at me.

"Hi," he said and smiled at me, advertising his dimples. "I'm Troy."

I said nothing, just continued to stare.

"You're the new girl, right?" the other man asked, holding out his hand.

I reached for it to shake, but instead he pulled me down from my post.

"I'm Connor." He smiled as he delicately shook my hand, staring into my eyes as if trying to find something—or like he had found something already. "What's your name?"

"I'm—"

"Petra Ambrosi," someone else said.

It was Ashton. I grimaced. I had known she would come see me sooner or later. She sauntered up to us with her beautiful grin, and all the attention that was given to me quickly turned to her.

"Ashton!" Connor shouted as he rushed up to her and gave her a hug. All followed suit—except Troy. His eyes were still on me. I ignored the urge to return his gaze.

Ashton walked up, wrapped her arms around my neck, and held me tightly for a while.

"Connor fancies you," she whispered in my ear. Her warm breath sent shivers down the left side of my body. She then released me to look into my eyes. "That makes two of us," she said, softly brushing her fingers across my cheek. The shivers spread instantly throughout my whole body, and my blood rushed to my neck and face, making me blush embarrassingly.

"Hey, Petra! We need you to come with us," Connor said, smiling at me. "We need your help painting the interiors of Resident Village."

I quickly shook the chills and blush from my body and face. "Don't I have to stay and lifeguard?"

"Don't worry. The kids don't need a lifeguard. Their counselors can watch them," he said.

I looked at Ashton, a bit confused, and she gave me a big grin back. "It's true, you don't need to stay here." She laughed.

I shook my head with a smile. "Whatever you say."

We left the pool house and started across campus, Ashton walking next to me, oddly quiet. I felt her eyes on me every so often. And it wasn't just her gaze I felt, but Troy's as well.

"Hey, you guys look alike!" Connor's head was on a swivel, looking back and forth between Ashton and me.

Ashton laughed. "Shouldn't we be used to this by now?"

I merely smiled. Although we had similar features, we had completely different personalities. Ashton's presence was very strong when she entered a room, and for that reason, she reminded me a lot of Apria. It was not because of her beauty—although Ashton was very beautiful, and mysterious, and, well, downright majestic—but because of her pride. She was confident, but in the humblest of ways. How she successfully juxtaposed the two was beyond my comprehension.

We reached the pathway that split the two rows of townhouses and retraced the steps I had taken many times with Taylor.

"We have to finish painting all the rooms in each townhouse tonight or I won't hear the end of it from Theia," one of the girls said. I could tell she was the leader.

Her features were sharp and thin, and her body was toned with broad shoulders. She wore her long black hair pulled back in a ponytail, and as she walked, she swung her big ring of keys on a Regis lanyard.

"Let's split into groups. Ashton, you go with the new girl, and Troy, you go with Connor. Let's meet back outside when we're finished," she ordered, and then hurried toward the first townhouse with the remaining girl.

Ashton grabbed a paint bucket, a pan, and a roller from the pile of supplies and started toward another townhouse. "Come on," she said, smiling.

I collected the identical tools and followed her inside.

"Let's start with the upstairs bedroom," she said, and then winked at me.

As we climbed the stairs, my nerves clouded my ability to read her emotions. I didn't even have nerves before! When we entered the bedroom, she crossed to one side of the room and set down her paint bucket as I went to the other side and simply stared at mine. After a minute or two, I glanced over at Ashton and saw her pouring paint into the pan. She then dunked her roller in until it was soaked thoroughly with paint and began to apply it to the wall. I copied her, rolling my brush against my wall.

Instantly, I felt her eyes boring into my back. I closed my eyes as if to shut her out. The bedroom began to feel very tiny, as though the walls were closing in on me.

"You don't know what you're doing, huh?" she said and chuckled softly. She was closer now, right behind me. I could feel her warm breath on my neck.

"Yes, I do," I said, answering the wall because I didn't want to face her.

Her lips brushed my skin softly as she moved even closer. I gasped. My nerves were back in full force, alive, warm, and tingling. Her lips brushed the back of my neck once more, teasingly. I stood still, and then, although I didn't want to, I turned to face her. I felt her excitement and closed my eyes to try to restrain it. What was she doing to me? I opened my eyes again and she smiled. She needed to stop that.

"You're scared," she said softly.

It wasn't a question. She knew what I was feeling. It was as if she had stolen my gift only to use it against me. She knew what she was doing to me. Was this what it felt like to be seduced? She was a predator toying with its victim—and if I allowed even a sliver of my vulnerability to show, she would pounce. I knew it all too well. I had used the same tactic in the past.

I stared at her for a long time and she stared right back. Soon enough, I started to see a color of hers that was so true, so sure. It was there, hidden beneath her words. She was lustful.

And me? Am I scared?

And then I answered my own question—I was curious. Curious about what she might do and what I might allow.

Suddenly, I had the feeling I didn't want to be alone with her anymore. I stared at her lips as she continued to talk. What was she saying? I couldn't hear anything, my attention focused on her lips more than her words.

"…Allison…"

That name snapped me back into focus. "What?"

"I said that I acted the same way when Allison approached me," she said, still smiling. *Why was she smiling?*

"And in what way is that?" I asked.

23

"Scared." She paused and then leaned in closer to me, pinning me against the wall I had just painted. I felt my back press against the wet paint as I prayed frantically for more room.

"The hard part is over," she said. "We've already kissed... But that's not why you're scared now. No, you're scared because you liked it."

She said it confidently, but I could feel her not yet convinced. There was still doubt in her mind about what I was feeling. With all my strength, I tried to settle my nerves. My strategy was to focus on Ashton and *her* feelings. Quickly, I ducked under her arms, releasing myself from her intentions.

She was truly a powerful seductress. Did she have the ability to seduce any God or Goddess of her liking? And how did she know my feelings? Was it because we were the same? I looked inward, trying to see if she was right, if I was truly scared.

I had felt fear when I thought I'd lost John to Hades forever. But I was not feeling that emotion at this moment. I wasn't scared. No, I was enthralled. More than ever, I wanted to know who Ashton was.

"You don't scare me, Ashton," I said.

"I don't?" She pondered my statement.

"No," I said, shaking my head. "You fascinate me."

She crossed her arms and smiled. She seemed to like that answer. We stood staring at each other for a beat.

"What am I to you?" I finally asked.

Her face was blank. I felt her searching for an answer. "I-I don't know. I feel like you understand me. I feel like I can tell you anything." She took a step closer, and then paused once I was against the wall again. "And," she said, leaning in, "I really, really like kissing you."

Her hand touched the bottom of my chin and pulled me close to her mouth. Our lips touched once again, and the thing that I didn't want to happen did. A thick wall fell away between us as I parted my lips to welcome her tongue. As my tongue touched hers, I thought I would be greeting passion, but instead her movements were soft and slow, as if trying to take in the taste of me and collect it in a memory. While I moved my tongue with hers, I was trying to figure out exactly whose wall was falling—hers or mine? The kiss felt the same as our first, gentle and sweet, yet with something hidden beneath it. She pulled away and looked me in the eyes for a moment, then put both hands on my cheeks and kissed me one last time.

I wanted to cry as she let go.

How could there be so much sorrow in the sweetest kiss?

Chapter 3

Lust

All through the night I thought of Ashton's kiss. I put my fingers to my lips and felt the warmth from hers still there, and then blushed, remembering it all over again. I had an urge, a desire, for more. Though full of sorrow, her lips had enchanted me and left me at a loss for words—and feelings.

I was so lost. And the further I dug, the more lost I became. Therefore, I stopped myself from thinking of Ashton, or anything else, and let my mind slip into my dreams. It was warm there. I was somewhere other than Earth, someone other than an exile. I was on a journey. What that journey might be, I had no idea.

In my dream, I saw my feet running, taking me somewhere. I couldn't look up to see where I was going; only my feet and the ground beneath them were in sight. Suddenly they stopped moving, grappling with an unknown obstacle. A pain started in my toes and in my feet. An aching, hollow pain. It started to crawl up my lower legs, then my upper legs. Onto my hips and up my stomach, the pain grew, until I grabbed at my chest.

I scratched and tore at my skin, clawing at it as if there were a beast inside, until finally I tore it open.

It was empty.

Someone has taken my heart. Or have I lost it?

I had a compelling drive to find my lost heart and soon came to a place where the road forked into two separate trails. One led east toward the forest and another west toward the sea.

My alarm clock went off and I bolted up in bed. As I rubbed the sleep out of my eyes, I began to think about my dream, turning it over repeatedly in my mind. I didn't have a clue what it meant.

∞

I hadn't heard a word from Taylor after her last text about not forgetting her. She hadn't responded to any of the texts I'd sent her in response. I never stopped to consider that I was waiting to hear from her, but I suppose I was. With that thought, I felt two different emotions arise within me. I held my breath, for they were coming at me so strongly. One was a stabbing, gnawing pain and the other contrastingly appeasing. With my emotions conflicted, I didn't know how I felt about her silence.

Am I grateful? Am I saddened?

Indescribably, I was both.

The emotional assault took place so quickly, and just as quickly it passed. I was finally able to let go of my breath with a deep sigh. I scanned the pool area to see if anyone had witnessed my embarrassing emotional attack. Thankfully, no one had. I was not getting used to them, and they only seemed to be getting worse as the days progressed. In the back of my mind, I wanted to curse Taylor's name for starting this to begin with.

It was the third day into summer break, and the heat had already begun to rise to unbearably scorching. Work had been very eventful the whole day. There was a camp council gathering before dusk, and the crew and I were to set up the auditorium. It was going to be huge; we had over twenty camps staying with us and more than 200 campers and counselors from each camp. Theia had all of her employees working the event, each paired up, and my partner was Troy.

During the free time between shifts, I had been getting to know the crew a little better. Connor was always very polite and charming to me. He was not bad looking either—tall, dark, and lean. He was also quite the humanitarian, and I think that was what I admired most about him. The two girls on the crew were inseparable. With the help of Ashton's insinuations, I realized they were companions and held a special bond that only they could understand.

I didn't know anything about Troy Thompson, though. He hadn't said one word to me or even looked in my direction since we'd first met. I wasn't surprised. He was an Athlete God. Their gifts came with arrogance, and I was not in any mood to try to befriend him.

We worked alongside each other the whole morning without speaking. It was just like any other day, but this time it was just him and me, so it felt more obvious. I couldn't feel him either, so I went off his body language, which made it appear that he was annoyed. He would stiffen up every time I was within a few inches of him. I began to get annoyed myself, so I stopped what I was doing and finally opened my mouth to speak to him. Then I saw Ashton approaching us and blushed instantly, remembering our kiss.

The day before at Resident Village, I had seen another side of her, and I think I liked it even more. She was a lion, and my reaction to seeing her today had me realizing that I had most certainly surrendered to be her lamb. It was my wall that had fallen.

"Can you come with me?" she asked, looking at me intently.

Without waiting to hear my reply, she started walking, and of course, I followed. She didn't let up until she reached a huge willow tree at the edge of campus, near the soccer field. She walked beneath it and sat, leaning her back against the trunk. She waited for me to sit too, and then paused for a moment before speaking.

"Do you like being here?" she asked.

Had she asked a couple of days earlier, I would have known the answer: I did not. I missed my home and my friends very much. Earth reminded me that I was in exile. However, in that moment, looking into her blue eyes, I searched for the answer. It was not easy for me to be on Earth, but I liked being there with Ashton.

"I like this," I said. "You being here with me."

She gave me an honest smile. She liked that answer very much. "I wish we could have this forever," she said softly, looking down at her lap.

Her reply sent a small shiver down my spine. "Why can't we?"

She turned to look at me. Her face wore a solemn expression that scared me. "Lust does not last forever," she said quietly.

I didn't understand. Was there something I'd missed, or something I hadn't yet seen? Was lust behind it all?

Her emotions erupted into my thoughts. She felt like crying. I cradled her cheek in my hand and held it there to catch her falling tears.

"I'm sorry," she said, embarrassed. "I've never been like this."

I was indeed surprised to see her vulnerable. I didn't know what to say, so I didn't speak, only watched her trying to hide her tears. There had to be another reason why she was sad, an unspoken reason hanging heavily in the air.

"What's wrong?"

It took a couple of minutes, but she finally turned to face me. She looked into my eyes, and with her stare my limbs fell limp. Her eyes were glistening from her tears, which made them even more beautiful. I forgot that I was trying to console her.

"Petra, I have to go," she said.

"I don't understand."

"It's my turn," she continued, "to be . . . judged."

The last word stung me like a scorpion's tail and made me swallow the breath I was about to take. The word was a poison. She did not look me in the eyes, instead looking down, away from me, her hair covering her face. She felt weak, as if all her energy had been sucked dry.

"I meet with the Moirai at midnight. I'll be gone for a week."

I didn't know anything about the judgment trials with the Moirai, but I hadn't thought it would take that long.

"A week?" I asked. "Why does the trial last so long?"

"It takes a week on Earth," she said, sniffling, "but less than a handful of minutes in the Heavens. Time does not exist where the Moirai are."

"Oh."

"If they see my destiny has not changed, they will send me to Tartarus immediately."

I saw the fear in my eyes through hers. My body wanted to cling to her in the hope that the Moirai did not take her. I wanted to run away with her and hide, but I knew neither of those were possible. I missed her already.

I closed my eyes and silently began praying for the salvation of her destiny. As I finished, I realized it was an odd prayer. I'd always thought destinies were certain and unchangeable.

"How does one's destiny change?"

It was a rhetorical question, but Ashton answered anyway.

"It's only the Lambdas' destinies that are unclear and changing," she said. "And there's great controversy over it. Some say the Lambdas are the creators of their own destinies. Others think the Lambdas do not believe in destiny, that everything is by chance, and therefore, there is no destiny to see. Whichever myths are true, the Lambdas' violation and penalty is all the same; they have disobeyed the rules of our great Zeus, and for that they are to be sent to Tartarus."

My stomach churned.

"I don't want to think about it now," she said, and I didn't try to argue with her.

As the sun started to set, we moved out from under the willow tree and sat again to watch the sky in silence. I tried to push away my racing thoughts, not wanting to believe it might be the last time we watched the sunset together. Suddenly, an uninvited tear ran down my cheek. She noticed, and I couldn't help but slowly let more fall.

She didn't question my tears, and I felt she understood them. Her hand was soft as it slid into mine. I held it tightly.

"Can you stay with me tonight," she asked softly, "until I go?"

At that moment, there was nowhere else I would rather be, so I nodded.

She stood up, still holding my hand, and looked at me as she lured me back under the willow tree. It was a look I would never forget.

We cuddled in the grass under the weeping willow's branches as the full moon cast its rays through the leaves, giving me just enough light to see her face. She reclined on one elbow, holding her head with one hand as the other rested on my stomach. There was barely enough wind for a chill, but my body shook with nerves. She saw, leaned in, and gave me a soft, gentle peck on my lips. Suddenly, my nerves calmed, and she smiled.

There was something beautiful in the way Ashton kissed me. A small peck left me unsatisfied, hanging in a fantasy of fascination. Her mouth was a bewitching tease holding me under a spell as it lingered on my lips. I didn't like the feeling, though I could not help but want more.

She leaned in once again and this time held her kiss a bit longer. I was still unsatisfied. I wanted even more. I think she saw it in my eyes, or my lips gave it away, because her arm went around my waist and she pulled my body into hers. As she pressed her mouth against mine, my body ignited. Hers did as well. We felt it together, and without saying a word, we started to undress each other in a rush, unveiling all the sacred parts of our bodies. I stared at her figure under the moonlight and saw how it resembled mine. Although they looked alike, her body held more knowledge and experience than my own. I felt shy but eager, innocent but curious. My body had much to learn from hers, so I allowed it to.

I felt my body move with hers as waves do, dancing a compelling dance. The dance ignited a sudden spark of its own, and as we danced faster and faster, the fire growing bigger and bigger, until finally, it reached as high as the moon. The dance broke as my body lifted to the moon's face and exploded into the stars. The fire was suddenly out, and I was left amazed by the beauty of the dance we had created. She smiled an open smile while exhaling deeply. She was there with me. Dripping and satisfied.

Once my exploding pieces fell back to me, I felt something unnerving about it all. My thoughts were erratic, and I was tired and breathless. I kept trying to think as I sucked oxygen back in. Something bothered me deeply, terribly. I lay by her with my eyes wide open, as exposed as her bare chest. They had never been more open.

No good will come from this. She may have been right. Is this not love?

I almost spoke the question aloud, but it stopped and stuttered on my lips, making them tremble. I began to see it clearer than the starlit sky: Ashton had had my body for the night, but not my heart, which was still missing. With that conclusion, I was overwhelmed by an unnerving new feeling.

"Allison met with them a week ago," Ashton said. The name drew me out of my thoughts and shot pain deep into the center of my core. "She gets back soon. Once she comes back, can you do me a favor?"

Allison was the answer. The unnerving feeling was betrayal. I had betrayed Allison. Immediately, I was ashamed. It would tarnish my loyalty and honor with Allison if she found out what had happened between me and Ashton.

I nodded.

"Can we never tell her or anyone about this?"

I was relieved, but my mind cringed thinking of the torment a secret holds.

"Never," I said.

Chapter 4

Second Chances

I awoke the next morning nude and alone under the willow tree, feeling sick over her leaving and what we had done. Nothing could be undone. And yet, even if I had the chance, I still would do it all over again. This was my inner turmoil: my body was satisfied, but my mind was not—nor my soul. What had I done? Something beautiful had happened to my body last night, but it was a wretched act to my mind. At least my body and mind agreed that something was amiss. Was this the power of lust?

∞

Whenever alone, my thoughts worked on me tediously, which made work more exhausting than ever. The empty time made my mind and body rise in a never-ending battle. I sat at my post twiddling my thumbs. Yet again, I was alone with no one to talk to. And even if I'd had someone to talk to about this, I knew I shouldn't, especially about what had happened under the willow tree.

The pool was empty, and I was actually glad that Ashton wasn't here. Now that she was out of sight, my body had forgotten what her touch was like, easing my mind. I could feel her enchantments beginning to wear off as the day progressed. I hated that every time I saw her, my body wanted her every attention. With her away, I could finally focus.

Through the pool building, I heard the echo of the door opening and instantly felt heat rush to my head, thinking the visitor might be Ashton.

"Petra?" a voice said. The heat vanished.

"Allison," I called back.

She walked up slowly, and then casually leaned on my post. "Did you miss me?"

I laughed and hopped down. "Tell me everything."

She smiled. "Come with me."

I followed her out of the building, across the schoolyard, and toward a hiking trail. As we walked, I tried to prepare myself for her news. I was excited to see her here and not in Tartarus, but I felt something heavy with each step we took. We didn't exchange any words until we reached the boulder where we'd first met. She sat on the gigantic stone and I followed right behind her.

Her eyes stayed forward, looking over the whole town as I looked at her with all the interest in the world, waiting for her to speak. She blinked a couple of times before smiling.

"I was given a second chance," she said finally.

I sat solemnly still. She breathed in a deep, tranquilizing breath and then smiled. "I'll tell you everything, Petra, everything. It'll be hard to understand it all."

I sat forward to face her, feeling her fervent spirit as she began to tell me about her trial.

"It was scary at first. I was at home sleeping, and the next thing I knew I was in a dark place. Everything was dark and quiet for a moment. Then a hand grabbed mine and the light drowned out the darkness. I saw myself standing, holding the Messenger God's hand. He held it very tightly, protectively, as we both looked forward into the light.

"I followed his instructions; he said wait, so I waited. He told me to stay calm, and I stayed calm. Then he squeezed my hand. With that sudden pressure, a flash of gold appeared. He was gone, but in front of me was Zeus. Beside him were the Moirai, the three Goddesses of Fate: Eunomia, Eirene, and Dike. They were beautiful, like three suns of beauty.

"Zeus did not say a word yet, just stared at me with his gleaming eyes. I had never seen such a celestial God before. He was everything we heard about growing up; huge like a giant, his body shining like a thousand suns.

"When the Moirai sisters spoke to me I couldn't move. I felt as if I were swinging in their array of order. Moreover, I didn't care. I felt nothing but warmth. Their voices—their voices, Petra, were the most eloquent tune to my ears. And only the purest of the Gods and Goddesses should witness what they spoke. I began to cry at their feet!"

I was at the edge of the rock as her story grabbed me closer. "What did they say?" I urged.

She smiled at my eagerness. "They said I had a second chance."

I felt the tears start to form in her eyes before I saw any fall. As she kept on speaking, they all fell at once.

"They said my future is something more than this, this imperfection. I will learn a way out of feeling *this* love."

I recoiled. "This love?"

"Lambda love," she said.

I sat back. "Lambda love," I whispered. "But, Allison, love is love. What's wrong with Lambda love if it is true?"

I stood up and pressed my feet into the boulder as I looked at her. As I stared, my nose started to tingle. The tears were building. *I cannot start this again. Not now.* But the water was rising under my eyelids, so I shut them before they could overfill. I had no explanation as to why I was so upset, but something about those words made my body hurt.

"Petra, they believe Lambda love isn't true love." She stood up and put her hands on my arms as if to try to control me. "Our Elders believe it to be ominous," she continued. "Our eyes are only seeing what is falsely there. Lust can only feel like love if it's been prevailed upon by evil."

I stared blankly at her, my eyes filling with tears. I thought of Ashton and me lying underneath the willow; lust was in the grass, in the glistening of the moonlight, in the weeping branches of the willow, and perhaps even in her touch.

Suddenly, an image of Taylor's face shot through my mind, and then I thought of our kiss.

"The Moirai saw that my future will come clear in time," she continued. "That I will make the right choice."

"Choice?" I asked, slightly peeved.

She smiled. "Then they vanished, leaving me with Zeus. He held his chin up to the stars for a while before he finally looked down at me. Then, very sternly, he said my time for tribulation had begun. If I choose the right way, I will be saved from Tartarus."

I gulped. "Choose?"

"To keep loving her or forget how to," she said with a small grin.

"Forget?" I asked, shocked and bewildered. "How does someone forget to love?"

A big grin began to grow on her small mouth. "Second chances, Petra. Thank the Elders for second chances."

∞

After meeting with Allison, I went back to the pool feeling as if I had no life in me. Her words rang heavily in my ears as I sat back at my post. My gut felt sick, and my mind was almost shattering with her words: *"Lust can only feel like love if it's been prevailed upon by evil."*

Was Ashton evil? How could the Elders say such things?

The Elders' aversion to love was spreading across the Heavens. Without even being there, I could feel it. Too many people had become Lambdas and then decided to rid their lives of love for strength in power. They were even teaching this to the students at Titanus.

Why? What is it that I cannot yet see? Is lust blinding me?

Allison sounded like Dion and Apria. Last winter, Dion had been branded with the Lambda because he had fallen in love with a God, and he and Apria had asked if I would share my gift with the young Gods.

Why does everyone want so badly to stop feeling emotions?

Dion and Apria had told me that the Titans were strong because they didn't have an emotional gene in their body. But in my eyes, they had ruled carelessly—raping, killing, and reaping anyone or anything they pleased. They had altered genetics in plants, animals, and even humans. They were the Gods, and no one could stop them. That was until Zeus and the Olympians did, of course. It was ironic to me; the Gods who overthrew the Titans now wished to be just like them. How pathetic.

With Ashton gone, I couldn't ask any of these questions. Her absence could not be any more of an inconvenience. I wished for Taylor to be with me and for her comfort. Her absence saddened and pained me as well.

What can Taylor be doing that is so important as to prevent her from talking to me?

Even though my heart didn't want to see it, this was a blessing in disguise. I supposed I needed to obey the Elders and forget her, too.

I only needed to make it through a few more hours of work, but my thoughts were running wildly. I needed a distraction.

I stared out over the pool and started praying to Poseidon. I prayed for him to strike the water and form a tidal wave to carry me far, far away. Perhaps somewhere isolated—nowhere near anyone. An island…my island.

Suddenly, Troy walked through the doors. Poseidon must have misunderstood me.

As he stomped closer, I felt him, tense and thoughtful. He was breathing heavily.

"Petra, can I talk to you?" he said curtly, his forehead wrinkling with his words. I watched him warily, and without saying another word, he unfolded before me, changing his demeanor into something less threatening. "I mean, do you have a minute?" he asked softly.

It was the first time I'd heard him speak since he'd introduced himself. His voice was deep yet calm, not alarming. How he said my name made me feel warm. It rolled off his tongue beautifully, even when sharply spoken. I looked out over the pool and saw no one in it. No activity at all, not even the tidal wave I had prayed for. I nodded to him.

He stopped a few feet from my post, looking up at me with his vibrantly blue eyes and failing miserably to hide his tension. I wondered where all his confidence was now. He hung his head and huffed lightly while shuffling his feet. Then he put his hands on his hips and sighed. I felt his turmoil; he didn't want to ask, but really wanted to at the same time. Finally, he stopped his nervous ticks and looked at me again, this time with solemn eyes.

"I was wondering if you were doing anything tonight?" he finally asked.

I began to smile, and worry quickly lifted his eyebrows. That was all he was conflicted about? I was blindsided, but relieved.

"I don't know," was all I could say.

His eyebrows relaxed, and then he smiled. He moved in a bit closer to my post and put his hands around the ladder as if he wanted to climb up, but then stopped.

"Would you like to accompany me tonight?" he asked. I could feel his sincerity.

"S-Sure" I said, shocked at the honesty of his request.

He smiled, and then said, "I'll pick you up before dusk?"

"Okay," I replied.

He smiled again and then nodded. "Okay."

He left with the biggest grin on his face. As soon as he closed the door, I let out the biggest gasp. There was never a moment where I suspected or sensed that he was interested in me. The times we were around each other were awkward and painful. Apparently, Troy thought otherwise. I had to smile at the thought, and hoped that I could begin to feel something *real* with him now that Taylor had awakened these emotions, but without the "ominous" feelings I had for Taylor. Could he be the distraction I needed? I gazed into the pool and fell into a trance.

Do I really want this?

Suddenly, I felt confused; I didn't know what I wanted. Just recently, my chest had opened up, the numerous emotions I'd never felt before in my life all blossoming at once. Now that I had them, I had a hard time getting rid of them. And did I truly want them gone? I was torn yet again.

Truth was, I *did* want these emotions, but not for Taylor, for the Elders forbade it. I had a choice this summer: to forget Taylor, or not to forget her and risk banishment to Tartarus. Whether I would forget her on my own or have help from Troy was what I had to decide.

As the serpent was to her prey, I felt the Moirai were to me. I could feel their breath on my neck, waiting for my choice. I began to pray to the one Goddess I had never prayed to before, for this was the first time I had ever felt the need to do so.

"My sweet Aphrodite, is there not a side of love that can grant me such a prayer? I feel it has abused its power before. But let it not do me wrong now, for I may have met my Adonis, and I wish to have feelings for him—and only him. Aphrodite, free me from this injustice and rid me of this wrong love. Let only the *truest* love find my heart and have our eyes find one another. And let our hearts beat together in a melody that only true love can create."

"Hello, Petra." A silky voice roused me from my prayer. She was lit by her heavenly glow and smiling beautifully with her sapphire eyes.

"Apria," I whispered. I smiled and hopped down to greet her. "What are you doing here?"

"I haven't heard from you," she said, innocently, "and you haven't been home."

I stared at her. *She doesn't know.* "I found a job here."

She watched me intently, but "Oh," was all she said.

Or does she?

"How did you know where to find me?" I asked.

She smiled and then gave me a dumbfounded look. "You're my best friend. I know everything about you," she said, laughing a beautiful sound.

"Does anyone else know?" I asked.

She gave me a sideways glance. "If you're speaking of your family, then no, no one else knows except for me and…" She paused and smiled. "Come, I have a surprise for you."

He was standing behind a big oak tree, trying to hide, but his glowing skin gave him away. I laughed, and he started walking toward me with a huge grin. As he came closer, a chalice formed in his hands from a cluster of vines wrapped around his wrist. He handed it to me, and I sipped the fresh wine made from his veins.

"So this is where you've been hiding," he said, smiling.

"Dion," I laughed, "I've missed you."

"But why, Pei? Don't you just love this place?" he asked, and then giggled.

"It's not bad. I'm trying out the mortal life and working here for the summer." I grimaced.

They looked at each other, and then looked back at me.

"You crazy celestial," Dion said, laughing. "Why in the Heavens would you want to do that?"

In that moment, I wished they knew what had happened to me. I had always been a horrible liar, and I could feel the strength within me ceasing to hold the lie. My stomach started to ache, my cheeks flushed within seconds, and then the feeling came. Fear. I stared at the pavement and prayed for my emotions to stop and for their eyes to stop watching me. Finally, my body started to get a grip on itself and I was able to lift my eyes to them. They were both glaring at me.

"Petra, are you well?" Apria asked.

"Is something wrong?" Dion said at the same time.

Their words shot through me.

Why am I scared to tell them the truth? They are my best friends; they will be there for me no matter what, right?

But then fear then swallowed my positive thoughts whole.

They will not love me if I tell them.

"I'm fine," I said. "It's just been a long day."

"Well then, drink up!" Dion slid his hand over the chalice and let the vines drip more of his sweet wine. One of the vines unraveled slightly from his forearm and unveiled his Lambda brand. A pain began to develop in my gut.

"So," Apria said, sipping from the chalice, "what exciting place shall we venture to today?"

38

"A trip?" I asked, suddenly excited.

Having my two best friends with me, as if nothing had changed, made me forget about my stomachache, Dion's brand, the Lambdas, and my exile.

"Here are our choices," Dion said excitedly, "Pillars of Hercules, the Devil's Sea, Aramu Muru, or Agartha—which I hear is lovely during this time."

The pain in my stomach reappeared. At the time of my banishment from the Heavens, Nick had told me I had to remain on Earth as I awaited my trial. Meaning, I could not leave. All the places Dion named were portals to the Heavens.

"Can't we stay here?" I asked.

Dion's head shot back and he looked at me with curiosity. "Okay, something's wrong," he said. "You love Heaven hopping."

I looked at them, and in that moment, they felt like strangers. I had to tell them.

"I can't go Heaven hopping," I said, shaking my head in defeat.

"Is there something you want to tell us?" Apria asked timidly.

It was the first time I'd felt fear from her. And the first time I'd felt my best friends as strangers.

Do I feel them as strangers because of this secret I hold from them, or is it me who is now a stranger to them because of it?

Suddenly, I needed to hold them closer to me, more than ever; and if the only way of doing so was to tell them, then they needed to know, even if they ended up hating me. Therefore, I swallowed my fear.

"I broke a law," I said, my voice as low as I felt.

I couldn't look at them. Feelings came at me, and I waded in each of them, one at a time. There was silence for longer than I wished. They were waiting for more words.

"I've done some things." I paused. They waited. "Lambda things."

Dion was suddenly beside himself, while Apria sat quietly.

"You're banished from the Heavens?" Dion asked.

"That is the real reason why I'm here and working," I said, my voice still low.

Dion looked at Apria as if she had an answer, and then looked back at me with a shocking grin. "The day has finally come."

Apria nudged his back, distracting me more than his words.

"What?" I finally let out.

"Dion," Apria gasped, and then gave him an irritable sideways glance. He recoiled.

"What?" I was alarmed and angry now.

I felt their shock more intensely than before. There was nothing right about their response. *They knew I would be banished from the Heavens one day? Was this the warning always saw in their eyes?*

"He meant we always knew your naivety would one day lessen," she said softly.

"Is that what it is?" I asked, pain forming in my eyes. "You two knew all along?"

Finally and quickly, my pain spilled out. I didn't try to hold anything back and began to cry. At their horrified expressions, my tears poured out more.

"I should have said nothing."

Neither of them reached out to me or consoled me in any way. Once I realized this, my tears began to dry. Never in our lives had they needed to console me. We sat looking at each other, not knowing how to react.

"Pei, you're scaring me," Dion said. I looked at him and his expression scared me just the same. "You can cry?"

I let out a weeping moan—a sound my lungs had never made before.

"Sit down, Petra," Apria urged me. "What has happened to you?"

Her question stung. "If only I knew," I replied with a sigh.

"Can you feel?" she asked with horror in her voice and every bit as much fear in her eyes.

"I can," I cried.

"What do you feel?" she urged.

"Everything," I whispered.

Dion finally grabbed my hand and pulled me closer to him. However, it was not to console me. He looked on my arms, lifting up my shirt to see my bare stomach and back, examining me down to my legs.

"She doesn't have one," he told Apria.

"I'm not branded," I said, "only banished—though equally humiliating."

Their emotions began to come to me as whispers. They were upset. I dug deeper, praying to find the answer as to why. I held onto Dion's arm, trying to gain a better sense. They were disappointed because now they realized I could not do what they had asked of me last fall.

"I can't help you guys," I told them.

"We realize that," Dion said, dismayed.

His look said everything. I caught Apria's eyes and had to turn away from them. They angered me more than I could even comprehend.

"Even if I still couldn't feel, I would not want other deities to be incapable of what I am feeling now," I said suddenly. "Everyone has a right to feel!"

"You don't understand the words you are saying," Apria said, her eyes refusing to meet mine.

"My words are from my own understanding. It is *you* who does not understand them."

Her sapphire eyes suddenly turned dark, a color I'd never seen before. "You speak out loud your ignorance like it is wisdom. Do not fool yourself, Petra."

Her words came as an electric shock and her condescension as a ton of bricks on my chest. She was angrier than I had imagined. Instantly, I felt she was hiding something again. But this time, her secret was more dangerous than concerning.

"What is going on, Apria?" I asked.

Dion stiffened, distress broadcast all over his body.

Apria did not look at me, and as the seconds kept passing, I thought she would never answer.

"A war is coming, Petra," she said, finally.

Dion gasped and started shaking his head disapprovingly.

I looked at them in disbelief. "Is this true?" I asked, looking directly into their eyes, one at a time.

I knew in that moment there was not even a sliver of doubt. Was this the secret they'd been keeping from me?

"A war?" I paused, searching their feelings once more. "With whom?" They were certain, and after sensing that, my voice began to tremble uncontrollably. "Ha--have you always known this?"

Apria shook her head as if to shake my questions away from her ears. "It's been seen by the Sisters of Fate that we are on the brink of one," she said softly, "but they haven't been able to see the adversaries just yet."

"Someone is trying to start war with the Elders?" I laughed. "With the Olympians? How is that possible?"

"It might be the Titans," Dion said cautiously. "They may have found a way to escape Tartarus and begun to build an army."

"The Elders think the Lambdas have a hand in it," Apria added.

Suddenly, as if the sky opened up, I felt the hidden pieces fall, land in front of me, and finally begin to take shape.

"That's why the Lambdas have been banished," I whispered.

They nodded slowly.

"The Lambdas can't be trusted until they've had their trials," Dion said.

"How long have you known about this?" I asked.

"We only learned of this from the professors at Titanus since your attendance at this mortal school," Dion said.

Then it had been several months. My stomach turned just slightly. It was such a heavy secret to be hiding from their best friend for so long.

"And this is the real reason why you guys came to me, asking me to share my gifts with the young deities—to prepare us for a war against the Titans, o-or Lambdas."

"Petra, you haven't seen what's been happening in the Heavens. Gaianus and this mortal school have kept you innocent," she said. "The Elders have lost control over the young deities. Their emotions are taking control, making them lose their minds. Some have fallen into depression, some into turmoil, and worse— suicide. The rate has increased dramatically just within the past several months alone. And emotion and love are the cause of it all."

"If only your own ancestor, Aphrodite, could hear you now, Apria," I told her. "Let them love. Love is never wrong."

She straightened, narrowed her dark eyes fiercely, and spoke with piercing words. "You have yet to feel love's evil, Petra. And I pray you never do."

Her eyes looked different from the eyes I had always seen growing up. These eyes belonged to another—one who scared me deeply.

"Both your brother and sister have stared at the end of Love's sword and been defeated. I don't have to remind you of Eva's journey to Tartarus or John's attempt at self-destruction."

Whether she intended it or not, the memory of my siblings' broken hearts came screaming back to me. I could hear Eva crying for her beloved just as I'd heard when I was young. I wanted to cry with John's conflicting emotions of suicide. Both of their hearts had had the final say; they did not want to keep living without their beloveds.

"As you have saved them," Apria's voice thankfully drew me out of the memories, "you will need to save other deities just the same."

"Do you see now, Petra, how important this is?" Dion asked sternly.

I did, and I slowly began to nod my head. But with the weight from the burden, along with the realization, my head slumped.

"I still can't," I said softly. "I feel now, and I can't enter the Heavens. I'm banished."

They gave no reply, nor did I have anything else to say. We sat in silence until finally Apria put her hand delicately on my shoulder.

"The young deities will have to do without for now," she said. "*We* will have to do without." She paused. "You need mending now."

"If the time ever comes for your judgment, I believe you will make the right choice. Just as I did," Dion said. He sounded far away, though he was merely an arm's length from me. *Choice.* I was relieved to hear it. My body let out a gasp.

"Is that why you're not banished?" I asked.

He nodded. "My judgment trial has passed."

"When?" I asked.

"This past spring."

I was sad to just now hear about it, but happy he was here. "Well, thank the Gods."

"Yes, thank them," he said. "Second chances."

"So I've heard," I said. "Then let the Gods hear my prayers with urgency. And commence my mending."

Dion began filling up the chalice once again, and we drank as we watched the sun set over the green mountains together for the first time in a long time. It was a great moment for me, a moment I wanted to save a little longer before night fell over us. We sat in silence together listening to the sky breathe. My spirit felt slightly lighter now that I had told them at least one of my secrets, and they had told me one of theirs.

We did not speak of the coming war, or my duty in helping the young deities. Apria was right; I was in desperate need of mending—forgetting—and soon, before the war began.

43

If I had the ability to give our Elders an advantage in a war, I would do it. And it meant I had to rid myself of these emotions once and for all and get back to being to my old self. That conclusion made me sad. The feelings of lust, love, fear, and happiness would all be gone. No more nerves or trembles from a kiss, no fear of wrong decision, nor the flips my stomach did when hearing someone had an interest in me.

"Troy!" I gasped.

Their heads shot up as I jumped to my feet.

"Troy?" Apria asked.

"I have to go. I have to meet someone."

As I hugged them and bid them goodbye, I ignored their unnerving feelings.

∞

I was an hour late meeting Troy at my house. I ran up the street, hoping he would still be there. Then again, I also hoped he wasn't. It would be easier to avoid him than to tell him why we had to stop before something even started. Though I was thinking too far in advance, it could go horribly wrong. He could not even like me—maybe he just wanted to hang out, or he could have already left to go back to the dorms.

I stopped several feet from my house when I saw him standing on the porch with Jaden.

He waited?

I walked up to them slowly. "Hey?" I called out.

He smiled. He wasn't mad. "Hey, I was getting scared. I thought something happened to you."

"Do you still want to hang out?" I asked.

He smiled again, making his dimples more pronounced. "Of course. That's what I've been waiting for."

Jaden was trying so hard not to burst out laughing, holding her hand up to her mouth.

"Jaden, would you like to join us?" I asked.

"No, I'm fine, thank you. But you kids have fun," she said sarcastically. I caught her smirk as she walked back into the house.

"Well, okay. Let's go," Troy said, and started making his way down the driveway.

"Where?" I called out.

He turned around and smiled, then beckoned me to follow. For a second I was still, not knowing whether to follow him or tell him I was tired and end the night. Lethargically, I watched his back as he kept walking down the street. He was in no hurry, but kept a steady pace that did not let up. I stared at him, my body fixed. I had to blink a couple times to adjust my eyes to what I was seeing. The streetlamps had not come on yet, making the residential road completely dark. Only, his glowing body lit the way down the street. I looked down at my body, which wasn't glowing as his was. By now I had gotten used to my body not having its glow anymore.

I started running to catch up to him.

"I saw you," I said finally, feeling more confident to approach the topic now that I'd seen his glow. "After you won a pentathlon event."

He kept walking without slowing his pace, but looked at me out of the corner of his eye and delivered a small smirk. His smile confirmed he was the Athlete God I'd seen paraded around by the crowd during the celebration. I kept looking up at him, waiting for him to respond, but he didn't. There was a long silence as we walked down the street and out toward the main road.

"How do you like your summer so far?" he asked suddenly, sounding a bit timid to ask.

His question surprised me. It came out of nowhere. My gifts felt like they were fading. Suddenly, I couldn't tell if he was being genuine or if he was mocking me. Did he know of my banishment from the Heavens? Instantly, paranoia started creeping up my back and into my head. I had to tell myself to relax in order to reply.

"It's okay." I looked up at him and caught him staring at me. His sincerity called my bluff and I sunk in my stance. "Though, I wish I were home. I don't like being here."

He laughed at my honesty. "Then why don't you go back?"

Was I going to have to lie to everyone? "I guess I'm here to live among the mortals and work as they do," I said, as though reading a part.

"Why are you trying to live with the mortals?"

I looked at him, once again surprised by his question. "Why not? Aren't you?" I shot back.

"No, not exactly…"

"Why then?"

"I like to explore and travel," he said. "I mean, don't get me wrong, I love the Heavens. It's a unique and beautiful place, but I would love to see more. I like all the ongoing changes this world delivers. I find this place fascinating. People here are always learning and evolving into something greater than they once were." He stopped walking, and I did too. "Look around you Petra; can't you see its beauty?"

I stared into his eyes a little longer, amazed to hear him speak. It was the most I had ever heard him say. I looked away finally, and did just as he said, looking all around me, and then underneath me. We were floating on a single cloud, going higher into the starlit sky. Once we were high enough, we hovered over the city of Denver. He was right. It was beautiful. The city lights reflected the hovering stars as if they were touching one another in greeting. It was beauty at its finest. For that moment, I did see it in a different light—his light.

We sat there for what seemed like hours. He slowly reached out and slipped his hand into mine. I hesitated and thought of pulling it away. I didn't understand what I was thinking or feeling, but I let him hold my hand for his pleasure.

As we sat looking at the imperfect beauty, we allowed time to pause and watch with us as the stars kissed the Earth's lights. I wanted to save the moment, but all I could do was smile; I was happy.

Chapter 5

The Balancing Act

"What's your name?" I asked.

My hand played with the sand as it fell through my fingers. She wore a white tunic with a hood covering her face. As she stood up, her shadow was cast upon me. She was taller than I was, and older, almost a fully grown woman.

As she ran down the shoreline, I noticed her body was glowing like a full moon. She turned around and beckoned me to follow. I found her footprints in the sand and placed my right foot in her right print then my left foot in her left one. Her feet were bigger than mine by a few inches. I stared at my feet in her prints until the water brushed over them and they vanished.

I looked up and found her kneeling in front of me. Her hood made her face dark, but glowing through the darkness, I saw the sea—her eyes were one and the same with the ocean. No one could forget eyes like hers even if they tried. She spoke a question, but in a tongue not familiar to my ears.

I shook my head.

Her eyes like the sea turned sad beneath the darkness of her hood, and I felt sad too.

"How old are you?" she asked in my own tongue, but broken.

I shrugged, and while trying to guess, I put up several fingers, then all ten of them.

"Where are your mom and dad?" she asked and then smiled.

I didn't know the answer, which made me sadder than before. "Deceased." I shrugged.

∞

My eyes shot open and I sat up. I checked my surroundings and realized I was not on the beach, but in my bed.

What a realistic dream.

I rubbed the sleep out of my eyes and looked out the window. It was still dark outside.

How long was I asleep?

The dream had awoken my mind. It wanted to do something. My eyes were still half-open when I reached out and caught the pen as if it had jumped into my hand, ready and willing to do whatever I wanted it to. I grabbed the nearest sheet of paper and started writing.

My heart is filled,
to where it may likely spill.
I cannot grasp the words that will come out.
What is it that it wants to shout?
O' Gods, I can barely breathe,
for my chest it seethes.

Though my heart vies with my mind,
which shall I choose to speak this time?
Can this hide before the peak?
Before it pounds right out to speak?
Hide away, poor vexed heart, I pray,
away from light and into dark to decay.

O' God of Justice, what was my crime,
to put such a horrid curse on this soul of mine?
Is it Love that has embraced me in her arms?
That took my gifts and all the same charms?
Or is it the other which prevails,
pinning my heart with hammer and nails?

Then hide, hide away, such foolish heart.
Do not come out until you spark.

My hand lifted from the paper, shaking like an aspen in the wind. I stared at what I had just written, stared at my hand as if it were not of my body but had a mind of its own.

Who is this about? Ashton or Taylor?

I held the pen tightly, hoping it would give me the answer if I squeezed it hard enough. I lay back down in my bed with my eyes wide open until my alarm went off.

I had lost sleep as well as my right mind—if I'd had one to start. Again, perhaps this was part of the buildup: the tension in my chest, the fear of when my judgment day would come. Would these emotions free me before then? Would I be able to revive before my tribulation—before this war?

I stood up from my bed, forgetting my alarm was still going off, and rushed to put on my work clothes. My new obligation fueled me. I had to forget Taylor Letto and close my chest before anything more happened.

I ran to my bedroom door and swung it open—and choked when I saw his green eyes. This time he was not wearing his infamous fedora, or any kind of hat. His dark curls hung loose over his brow and ears, and his grin was dark in the shadows of the early morning. He looked huge, covering the whole doorway with his arms up, holding it on each side with his winged sandals dangling loosely from his fingertips. He seemed a bit out of breath, as if he was in a rush.

It must be time. Why else would he be panting at my doorway?

"Nick," I said in a whisper.

"Were you heading out?" he asked between pants.

"I have work."

"Work… right. How is that going?"

"I'm late," I said.

He held my gaze, tilting his head with curiosity as his panting slowly subsided. "I need a bit of your time."

I gulped. *This is it. It's my time. He is going to take me to the Moirai.* I took in a deep breath.

"Okay. Let's go."

"I'm here to give you a message."

I nodded for him to proceed.

"There's news about Ricky," he said quickly, his voice cracking on the name.

I closed my eyes to ward off my sadness, but the memories of Ricky came back: the day we first met, the day I broke his heart, our reunion at the Ten-Day Celebration, and his heart breaking all over again.

"It's happened to him too, Petra," Nick said. "He's done it... he went to Tartarus."

There was a dark cloud that I hadn't known was even there, hidden in its own dimension, that finally became known to my reality. My head screamed with uncertainty. Then, within a flash, the white room appeared before me. I shook my head, and the white room was gone.

"Is something the matter, Petra?"

I was back in my room, with my bed and desk, and Nick standing in front of me.

"No," I said, but I still felt cold.

I couldn't believe it. Eva, John, and now Ricky. Things were getting worse in the Heavens. There was no question though, no hesitation in my mind at all—I had to rescue him. It was my fault he'd broken.

"What are we to do about Ricky?"

"Save him," I said.

"Petra, I'm just telling you what's happened to him. I knew you two were close..." How did he know that? "And besides, you can't leave Earth..."

His voice sounded far, echoing through the pale walls. Then suddenly, I didn't hear his voice anymore. I was back in the white room—in the Underworld.

"I can fly you to Tartarus, but..." a voice said.

Slight hums and mumbles were still coming from Nick, but I couldn't tune into them. I was in the white room, alone, scared, and confused.

"You will get into so much trouble," I finally heard him say.

His face appeared through the white walls. Then the walls around him turned into my bedroom again.

"I don't care," I said. "He doesn't belong there."

∞

We entered the Heavens' portal and landed a mile away from Mt. Tartarus. There was nothing around us except gray desert and gray skies.

"Okay," I said. "Now how am I supposed to get into Tartarus?"

"There are two entryways," Nick said, then added, "that I know of. There is the entry through the gates. But hydra-reptilians surround them, and the gates will only open if Zeus or Minos were to bring you. And you could only enter if Tartarus himself saw that your punishment fit the crime."

He paused and took in a deep breath. "But there is another way, a very secret way that I think will work for you. On top of the mountain, there is an opening. You can enter it easily, but that's not where the challenge lies. Once you enter the hellhole, fear—a great and horrifying fear—will overtake you. It is said that one faces their demons and loses their sanity. The fear is the challenge. It eats away at your will. However, *you* are the Goddess of Emotion who cannot feel, so this will be easy for you!" He slapped me on the back. "All you have to do is remain focused on what you are there to do. Focus on Ricky."

Great. If he didn't know already from consoling me a couple weeks ago, then I didn't want to tell him I could feel now. I wasn't sure if it would harm anything, but I thought it better not to tell him at this particular time.

"So, how am I supposed to enter the mountain's roof?"

Nick smiled instantly. "My sandals." He took them off and handed them to me. "Okay, Petra, so to begin flying, you have to start running really fast…" I put the sandals on and started running before he finished, but Nick kept on with his instructions as I began ascending, "And you can't take off unless you jump really high!"

"Petra, be careful!" he yelled as I made my way toward the mountaintop.

I reached the opening, which was no bigger than the trunk of a redwood tree and glowed with Hades' fire. I fell through the hellhole without thinking twice, without thinking about how I would get back out, and without knowing if I could ever leave. I needed to save Ricky even if it meant risking my own life. I could never leave him to be tormented in Tartarus because of my actions.

The wings on Nick's sandals were out, gliding me down the hole. Immediately upon entering, darkness and cold swallowed me. My feet hit the ground so hard my body crumpled, and I rolled forward. I slid to a stop. The ground between my fingers was layers of ash, pumice stone, and bones, and the smell was no better. The air was atrocious, poisonous, smelling like burning hair, skin, and mold. Smoke and gas rose from small holes everywhere in the ground. I did not want to breathe in, so I held my breath, only gasping every minute or so.

I looked around, trying to find somewhere I could begin my search, but as far as my eyes could see, there was nothing but pitch black in every direction. I closed my eyes, took in a deep breath of the horrific air, and started walking forward.

It didn't feel like such an awful place. Not compared to the reputation Tartarus had, at least. Apart from the darkness and the rotten smell, it wasn't half as bad as Hades.

I must have gone a mile or more without reaching anything but more darkness. I wondered if there was an end to the prison, or if I had gone in the wrong direction. So I turned around, back to where I'd come from. It mirrored where I had been walking. I turned around again, and then again. I was lost, no longer knowing which direction I had come from or where I was going. Very soon after, I felt the fear began its sinister crawl up my body and into my mind. I didn't want the fear to succeed, and I knew I needed to make it stop; thinking of the fear only fed it, making it grow. Instead, I thought of Ricky's face the last time I'd seen it, and his silver blue eyes and smile quickly appeased me. I thought about his laugh, and the things he'd do to make me laugh. He was always kind to me and did anything for me. I missed him.

Suddenly, a tiny sliver of light breached the darkness above my head. I looked up and took a few steps back to see better. As my eyes began to adjust, I saw the shadows of something hanging from a darkened ceiling. The light slowly began to grow, spreading its glow around the hanging object. Finally, the light revealed the object, and I gasped loudly.

Ricky's lifeless body hung above me. What his body was hanging from, and where it was hanging made me gasp even louder, and my voice echoed throughout the space. The sight was almost unbearable. His body was bent backwards with a gigantic hook piercing clean through his chest, like a fish caught in a fisherman's hook. I was thankful for the tears in my eyes, for they blocked out most of what I was seeing. His heart couldn't have been beating. I doubted if he was even alive. Then suddenly, just like a fish, his lifeless body flopped.

"Ricky!" I shouted.

He stopped flopping and allowed his body to bend back more so he could see where I was.

"Petra?" he whimpered.

"Oh my Gods, you're alive!" I cried. Hope came to me then like fire in a winter storm. "I'm coming," I yelled, and backed up so I could get a running start.

"No!" he shouted.

I shuffled my feet and then stopped. "Wha-what?"

"No, Petra, don't!" he yelled again.

I ignored him, and without thinking twice, backed up and started to sprint. The wings caught flight again, and I quickly made my way up to him. I soared over and around Ricky until I caught hold of the hook's neck. As I hovered over him, I couldn't hold back the tears.

"What have I done," I whispered.

With all my might, I lifted Ricky's body. I didn't know where my strength came from, but I was sure to thank the Gods. This must be fate if they were helping me. As soon as I unhooked him, I focused on the sliver of light that had breached the darkness. I hoped it was the opening to the mountain.

"Hold onto me tightly."

Ricky looked at me, hesitant.

"Ricky, grab onto me!" I yelled, and this time it was a demand.

He finally motioned to me, but too slowly, so I reached out and grabbed his arm and put it around my waist.

"Hold on tightly," I said.

He did as instructed. I let go of the hook and felt us begin to fall. I pedaled my feet as if I were running on air. It worked, and the wings flung out of the sandals and started flapping.

We shot through the hole and into the gray sky. I wanted to kiss such an ugly sky, for it was the most beautiful thing my eyes could behold after the darkness of Tartarus. I landed with a hard thud, and Ricky quickly let go and fell to the ground.

He said no words, only looked at me with staid eyes. I stared back, waiting for him to do something, say something. Finally, he did.

"What have you done?" His voice was a soft yet brutal whisper.

I stood up quickly, his words pushing me like hands. "I—"

"I wasn't supposed to be saved, Petra."

"But I saved you," I said softly, "from your broken heart."

"No," he stared deep into my eyes.

At that moment, I was more frightened than when I was down in Tartarus. He slowly lifted a flap of his bloodied toga, revealing his arm. He held it out, showing me the Lambda symbol branded deep into his forearm. My eyes swelled and my mouth fell open.

"What *have* I done," I whispered in understanding.

53

"I was *sent* to Tartarus, Petra," he said softly.

At that moment, I felt Nick behind me. At least I wasn't alone; I felt his shock even before I saw his face.

"Ricky," Nick's voice trembled, "why?"

I was thankful to see Nick shocked. There would have been many questions as to why he'd had me risk my life to go to Tartarus and save a Lambda from his own conviction.

"It doesn't matter," Ricky said.

"The Messenger God has been given the wrong message?" I asked aloud, my voice surprisingly calm. I slowly turned my head to face Nick and felt his shame wash over me.

"No," he said softly. "Ricky is my best friend. I wanted to save him for my own benefit. No Elder knew about this." His voice was low and reluctant.

My own voice came out unexpectedly shrill. "Oh what a hero! Having me risk my life instead of your own."

"Had I known he was *sent* there and not gone because of a broken heart like I was told, I would have never risked any lives," Nick said. He didn't dare to look me in the eyes, but his shame washed over me once more. I had given him enough grief; his shame was doing more of the damage anyhow.

"So what will happen now?" I asked. "The Elders will know soon enough…" My voice trailed off. I was distracted by the terrifying expressions Nick and Ricky's faces were making. Ricky then jumped to his feet and Nick began to stammer.

Simultaneously, they both screamed, "Petra! RUN!"

Run? I turned around to see what they were looking at.

They were as big as giants and had bulging muscles like rhinoceroses. They wore titanium helmets with onyx horsehair sprouting from the top. Their coal black capes and tunics were thick and shredded, as if they had come from battle. They wore titanium sandals, leg guards, and chest plates that blinded my eyes. And they came running, fiercely, at us. The ground shook as they came closer. There were twelve of them, and each one held silver weapons in their hands as if they were about to fight off Cerberus. I knew who they were from their dark eye sockets, looking like huge, fearless ghosts: Heavens' Guards.

"RUN, PETRA!" Nick and Ricky shouted again.

One of the guards stopped and prepared its bow. I watched it notch its arrow, stretching the string as far as it allowed, and then aim—at me. With the release of the archer's fingers, the arrow flew straight. I looked the flying arrow dead in the eye. That was when I decided to run.

"Oh sh—!" I yelled.

"RUN!" the boys screamed again.

As fast as I could, I ran in the opposite direction. Then suddenly something that felt like cuffs clenched tightly around my wrist. I looked up and saw Nick.

"I have you!" he called down to me. "I won't let them take you!"

My body felt his doubt in spite of his confident words. Then I saw he was holding Ricky in his other arm.

Great. I am in big trouble.

Chapter 6

Change

Fear fogged our minds. We couldn't think of a plan as to what to do with Ricky. Should we bring him back or hide him? Neither Nick nor I wanted him back in Tartarus, so Nick decided to hide him and wait for whatever consequence we got for taking him.

The whole trip to Tartarus only took a few hours, yet when I arrived back home it was already evening. I had missed a whole day of work.

I hadn't realized how tired I was until I slumped down on my bed. My body was exhausted.

I began thinking about the young woman in my dreams the night before. How it had felt so real. I thought about her eyes, which not only held the beautiful colors of the sea but also felt like gateways to her heart, giving me the gift to see her soul. I was still holding onto the belief that I had seen those eyes before. But where?

Sleep's hands began pulling me under, but then Taylor's face appeared, reviving me. My mind took hold of her lips, the lips that held all her desire. A fire that burned brighter than a sun but felt as soft as falling rose petals on my lips. I suddenly felt her body next to mine. It felt so real, as if she were with me at that instant. I wondered if she was dreaming of me, too. If someone, somehow, had found a supernatural link with another being. The kind of link that didn't go away, never to be detached, never to be broken—no matter the distance, no matter the time. And possibly, this link only needed to form once their eyes met.

As if seeing each other for the first time would link their souls for eternity—unconditionally.

∞

I slept in and arrived late to work the next day. Between missing work the day before and being late again, I was expecting to hear it from Theia or one of the crewmembers. But they were still gathered in the courtyard near the student union building, talking amongst themselves as I slowly walked into the conversation. Their faces were dirty and sweaty.

Connor slightly nodded to me, a bit out of breath. I spotted Troy next, just in time to catch his eye. He smiled and then looked to the ground, still smiling.

The building behind him caught my attention. The library. Quickly, thoughts of Taylor began to develop, but I yanked my eyes away before any of them could.

The veteran leader gave us our orders, and we quickly dispersed to start them.

"Petra." Troy's hand wrapped around my shoulder and turned me gently around to face him.

"Hey," I said, thinking about his hands and what I felt when he touched me. It was a nurturing feeling, but there was something else, something hidden under his fingertips.

"Where were you yesterday?" he asked through a big smile.

I thought about the day before, about my journey to Tartarus. "Busy."

I watched his expression.

"Oh," he said. "Well I was wondering if you had plans after work."

I was quiet for a bit, trying to read him. He began to squirm from my silence, stepping back and then quickly shoving his hands in his pockets. In that moment, I couldn't sense anything from him.

"I-I was just wondering if you would like to get coffee with me?"

After work coffee? That sounded harmless, nothing that indicated he would try to seduce me into loving him.

"Yeah," I finally said. "Okay, after work."

He nodded, trying to hide his smile. "Okay," he said with one last nod, and then walked away.

∞

I sat in our living room, buried deep in the cushions. Jaden was in the kitchen putting away dishes when she saw something through the window. She glanced back at me and smiled. I just sat and looked at her, beginning to feel like there was something wrong—not with her, but with me. I couldn't feel the reason for her smile.

"He's here," she said, still smiling.

My breath spoke with a cry because of that insensible smile. I stood quickly and felt fear on the back of my neck. We both turned to the knock on the door.

"Have fun, Petra!" Jaden laughed.

57

I opened the door and hesitated. Troy looked back at me with a big grin. I couldn't sense anything from him either.

"Hey," he said.

"Hey," I replied. "Let's go."

I walked past him, down to where I'd parked Jaden's bike on the lawn. I jumped on it and started pedaling down the street. Something was definitely wrong; they had to be feeling something when they were smiling. I peddled faster as my anger grew.

"Wa-Wait up!" Troy shouted, but I only peddled faster. "Petra! Wait up!"

This time his voice was a lot louder, but farther away. I looked back to see just how far and could barely make out his expression, let alone sense his emotions. His face changed. As my bike pulled farther away from his, I squinted to see his expression. It was terrified, and I became angry that I couldn't sense why.

"Petra! Petra, watch out!"

Her eyes flashed through the darkness. I smelt the sea, heard the birds and the waves crashing. There was a body lying next to me. Then everything flashed black again.

∞

I didn't feel anything at first, but I must have been hit pretty hard because I landed several feet from the car. I sat up and saw a man standing outside the car, looking at me as if I were a ghost—as if I were dead. I should have been. I lay my head back down on the pavement and for a moment, wished I was.

"Petra! Are you okay?" Troy ran up beside me and put his hand behind my head. He stared at where the blood dripped above my eye, and then at the big gash in my leg. "Wow, that's pretty deep."

He eyed it with a disgusted look when he saw my bone and muscle tissue coming out of the opening. When he took his hand out from under my head, it was covered in my blood.

"It should only take a moment before it heals," he said calmly. "We should go before it happens in front of him."

I quickly stood up and shook him off, trying not to look as if I was bleeding out from everywhere. I wiped the blood from my brow and stared hard at the mortal man who had hit me. He looked pale and sick, like he was going to vomit. I couldn't sense what he was feeling, and I wanted to hurt him for it. I stood crutched over Troy as I stared hard at the man's pale face.

What is he feeling?

I limped over to him, my pace quickening as my blood streamed out. Each limp I took, I felt myself getting angrier and angrier, but still nothing from the man. Nothing. I took a final step, and then everything went black.

∞

Words could not express it. I had never felt such pain before. It felt like Zeus had struck me down with his bolt and severed my body. Her eyes dropped tears behind the hood that covered her face. She looked up; the darkness still hid her well, but not her glowing eyes. They were so full of tears I could barely see the sea's colors in them. She held her hand on my cheek as I wept with her. She reached up and eased her other hand over my chest, to cover my heart. Her hand only soothed the pain for a moment, and as soon as she let go and stood up, it was as if she had ripped it out of my chest.

Why does this pain have to come from the organ you need most?

Her crying caused me more pain than her leaving. She gave me one last, gentle, passionate kiss before wading into the water toward a small boat and waving goodbye as she sailed into the sunset.

∞

My eyes slowly opened, and immediately the pain came. My head felt as if it had been ripped apart.

Am I still dreaming?

I couldn't think. The pain in my dream had felt just as real. It was the same woman as before, only I was older and she looked just the same, as if time had not worn on her body.

My mind was half-awake, but my whole body ached with an unbearable pain. There was a blurry, shadowed figure near my bedside. The young woman from my dreams? I prayed to the Gods for my vision to return, but only more pain came.

"Sleep, Petra," the shadowed figure said, "sleep."

"Are you feeling better?" a voice said.

My eyelids were heavy as I tried to open them and focus on the figure above me.

"She'll be fine. Look, it's already scarring. Give her some more water," another voice said.

"Sip this, Petra."

I did as the voice instructed.

The other figure took the cup from me. My eyes followed the hands and saw that they belonged to Jaden. Her brow was furrowed deeply.

"Here, eat more," said the other voice. Fingers held out what looked like jelly and smelled like sweet fruit. They held it delicately to my lips, and I tried to swallow. "Glad you're finally awake, Petra."

My eyes finally adjusted, and I saw who was feeding me. "Nick?" I never thought I would be so happy to see him. "How long was I out?"

"A few days," he replied.

I sat up in bed, taking in a deep breath. Both faces watched me intently. I felt a third body's tension and noticed Ricky in the corner. Slowly, I stood alongside my bed and immediately crumpled to the floor. The little pain in my head and body reminded me of what had happened. I looked down to the gash in my leg just in time to see the scar tissue disappear, until there was nothing left but brand-new skin. My breaths became shorter, and I started to pant. I needed air—and answers.

"What happened?"

"You were in a coma," Jaden said. Her head was down, looking at the empty cup. I felt her deep sadness.

"How?" I asked.

"You hit your head pretty hard," Nick said.

"How?" I repeated.

All of them looked at me with the same solemn stare. They knew what I was really asking: How did I get hurt when I was a Goddess? When I was immortal? I felt their reluctance to answer, and their distressed glares began to wear heavy on me. I got up and sat back down on the edge of the bed with my elbows on my knees and my palms clasped together as if I was praying to the Gods. The glowing from my hands caught my eye suddenly. It was light out, with the sun breaching the window, and I could see my body's glow.

"What did you give me?" I asked. With that, more questions unraveled in my mind. They all began to scream out at me, desperate for answers.

The three of them were still silent. I could feel their desire not to answer anything and began to lose patience with their silence. Heat rose instantly within me as my blood raced faster in my veins. I began the countdown in my head before the scream, before my mind exploded. *Three… Two…*

"ANSWER ME!" I cried out.

"You were becoming mortal, Petra!" Jaden announced in a shrill voice.

The room was hushed, and in that silence, I sensed her so easily. Her sadness and disappointment. *In what?* I sensed her harder and then I knew: she was disappointed in herself.

My eyes closed. I was on an island and saw a sailboat tied to a small dock.

I opened my eyes and felt a tear fall. Before I knew it, they all did; each tear racing the others down my cheeks and chin. I looked at Nick, Jaden, and Ricky individually, at their faces, and then at their eyes.

"How?" I asked once again, the question feeling repetitive on my tongue.

"We don't know," Jaden said softly. Her voice was raspy and broken; there in the cracks, dismay lay hidden. "There are possibilities, but nothing certain. Nick and Ricky found you ambrosia nectar, to test one of our theories."

So I had gotten my glow from the nectar of the Gods, which meant I was immortal and strong with my gifts again. However, with one question answered, I felt another turn over in my mind. Demigods and the Nurtured were the only ones given the nectar of the Gods; that could only mean one thing.

I could not make my tongue form the words. I looked back down at my leg. It was so beautiful and rejuvenated—a sight I had not seen since I'd started at Regis last fall. I looked at them with wet eyes.

"Petra," Jaden whispered. I wanted it to be her tongue to say it. Not mine. *Just say it. I need to hear it.*

"According to the scripture, only a mortal that has been given ambrosia by a God or Goddess can be granted immortality." She sat next to me on the bed, and then finally looked into my eyes.

I knew what she was thinking before her lips began to form the first letter. I knew what that meant. I knew that if a deity gave ambrosia to a mortal, it gave them immortality; what the mortal didn't know, but every deity in the Heavens did, was that to remain immortal, they would need to *keep* consuming ambrosia. Forever.

I began to sense her whole body and everything she was feeling. My powers were stronger than ever, alive, my senses acute, magnifying even the tiniest bit of emotion from them.

Everything came at me within that pause: Jaden was trying to remain calm, Nick was on edge, and Ricky was overwhelmed with tension. Each of them had a war going on inside themselves.

"Your father is a Nurtured," she said, "and your mother…" She shook her head. "But that's where I'm confused, Petra, because you're not a Nurtured. You're not like your mother and father." She sighed. "You were born a Goddess, not made into one. You are Petra Ambrosi, the Goddess of Emotion."

Her confusion was greater than my own. She let out a desperate sigh. "Petra, my duty is to protect you, and I have dishonored Poseidon, and you, by failing to do that when you were hit by the car. I give you my oath this will never happen again."

The disappointment and shame she felt sent shock waves into my chest. At that heightened moment, I felt the sincerity in her eyes; she really was here to help, and she really was someone I could trust.

"Do you accept my oath, Petra?"

I regarded her for a moment before answering. Within that pause, a different light shed upon her. The kind of light you look for in a friend—in a guardian, I suppose.

I nodded. "I do." I looked at her, into her eyes. "Then will you help me with something?"

"Anything," she replied.

"Help me find the truth. Help me find out who I really am—a Nurtured or a Goddess."

"I will."

Nick and Ricky moved closer, eying me, and then Jaden, and then each other.

"We were all talking," Nick said, carefully. "We're all curious about why this happened, Petra. We all actually would like to help you figure this out."

I felt my mouth fall open. It was kind of them. Unexpected.

"But why?" I asked.

Nick's lips curled back into a cheeky smile. He looked at Ricky, then to Jaden, and then back at me again, and gave a shrug. "Sounds like a mystery that needs to some solving?"

Chapter 7

The Plight

I was enjoying the alone time I spent working at the pool more and more every day. I liked having no one talking to me. I needed the time to think things over, to find the answers to my questions. Who was I? The Goddess of Emotion? A Nurtured? A Lambda?

"Petra!" I felt Allison across the pool before I looked up to see her. I smiled with all the enthusiasm I could fake. As she got closer, I braced myself for the news she was excited to tell me.

"Petra, I have good news— Whoa, look at you." She looked me up and down. "You're glowing!" Her voice echoed through the building.

I rolled my eyes and hopped down from my post, landing next to her. She kept smiling at me. I just shook my head.

"What's your news?" I asked, smiling.

"Well!" she said, "I've been talking to Taylor. We're thinking about living together!"

Allison's emotion was enthralling, yet mine went into a dark place, and my smile quickly faded. Like flint that sparked the fire, her name sparked something inside me. It was all I could think of as Allison continued talking.

Taylor has been talking to Allison?

I thought eating ambrosia had revived me—my glow was bright, my gifts acute—but I still could feel the grief I held for Taylor. When would I begin to mend?

"We're looking somewhere close to school, but we haven't found anything yet," Allison was saying.

Taylor hasn't spoken to me all summer, but she's speaking to Allison?

It just didn't make sense. Nothing made sense. I was thankful my head had instinctively started nodding, making it seem I was still listening.

"Ashton won't like this, but I hope she'll understand, *if* she gets back. I'm safe now. I have to stay on the right path."

But I could feel her holding onto Ashton still. She was just afraid to feel.

"If I lived with her then nothing would change. It would be as if we were still together. My emotions would win." She paused. "In order for a second chance, my new life has to be without loving her. … I can't love her."

Hearing her talk like that made me feel sick again. Her sadness crumbled her legs and she sat down in the chair next to me. I sat with her and waited for her to say more. But she was silent, trying to reason with the war in her heart.

"I think it will be good if I live with Taylor," she said. "I want to live with friends and have fun."

Her pain was intense now. I could nearly feel it as if it were my own. I wanted her heart revived and happy. I wanted it so much for her… almost as much as I wanted it for myself.

"You will," I said.

We will.

∞

I walked home kicking a rock I'd found at school. I watched it turn over on its side, lifeless, and stop rolling. I sat on the curb near where the rock lay in the gutter, wishing I had strength like the rock, like Allison. I admired her determination to overcome her love for Ashton. I admired her so much I envied her.

None of this would have happened if not for that stupid kiss.

The thought made me angry with Taylor, remembering how I'd received the emotions in the first place. I grew even angrier remembering Allison telling me she had spoken to Taylor.

What are her reasons for not talking to me? Just as I thought the question, I caught myself. *Why does just the mention of her name put my emotions in a frenzy?*

I should have been grateful. Too much depended on my mending. I needed to save the Elder Olympians from the coming war, and I needed to save myself from becoming a Lambda. I knew that just admitting any feelings I had would make it true that I had them in the first place. Therefore, I could admit nothing.

When I walked in the house, I immediately drank in Jaden's disturbing aroma. I followed the odor to its source and found her sitting at the kitchen table.

"What's wrong?" I asked.

She looked at me and started shaking her head. "I just heard from Britta," she said. "That damn mortal."

I gritted my teeth, sensing the news was discouraging. "Is she well? Did something happen to her?"

Jaden let out a high-pitched laugh, got up from the table, and moved to slump on the sofa. "She doesn't want to move back in with us when school starts."

"What?" I asked, joining her on the couch. "Are you certain?"

She nodded.

"Why?"

"She said she didn't feel comfortable living with us." Another laugh erupted out of her.

I sat still for a minute, processing the whole thing. Finally, a small smile curled my lips and I couldn't help but laugh with her. Soon both of us were rolling around laughing.

"We're too weird for the mortal!" Jaden shouted, giggling.

I laughed even harder and fell over onto the cushion next to her. I looked up at her, still giggling, but stopped laughing when I felt her emotion change.

"Hey ladies," a voice said.

Both of our heads shot toward the voice.

"Diane!" Jaden shouted. "What are you doing here?"

I kept still. It was odd for me to finally see Diane now that I knew who she truly was. I watched her mouth carefully as she spoke, as if every word was going to come out as a beguiling song.

"Hey Petra," she said, smiling sweetly.

I nodded, and then smiled. She was squeamish with her feelings. I felt her closely and only found urgency within her nerves. Her eyes fluttered to me, and then back to Jaden.

"Jaden, may I speak to you privately?" she asked.

They left the room and went down the hall. I went to the kitchen to fix myself some dinner. There were only a couple of things on the refrigerator shelves: many large containers of ambrosia, enough to last me until the end of next spring, and a half-empty bottle of wine. I thought about going to the market but quickly rejected the thought, remembering the last time.

Jaden came back into the living room holding a small chest that looked centuries old. My eyes followed her as she came over to me and set the chest on the counter.

"Whoa, what is that?" I asked, eyeing its beautiful carvings.

It was a red oak chest with bronze straps and fitted bronze locks on each of its sides. The locks had etchings of a small tree on them. It was very worn and rustic, as if it had been through a lot of harsh weather.

"Poseidon said it was yours."

"Poseidon?" My eyes widened.

"Diane said Poseidon gave it to her to give to you."

"Well, it's not mine. I've never seen it before."

I sensed that she was just as confused as I was. "Well just take it to your room. It's too ugly to be seen out here."

I laughed. "Is that all she came here for?"

Last school year we barely saw Diane in the house, although her things were still in her bedroom. I suspected the upcoming school year would be just the same.

"No," Jaden said cautiously. "She told me she won't be attending school this year."

"Is it because we're weird?" I asked, and we both laughed.

"No," she said somberly. "She was given different orders from Poseidon."

"Oh." We both sighed. "And just like that we're out two roommates," I concluded.

"Well then," she said with a smile, "let's start looking for two more."

Chapter 8

Just Friends

I stared at the chest across my room. It was past midnight and I couldn't beg my eyes to close. As time kept passing, I thought about what I should do with it. I was intrigued about its contents, though I had to consider the chance that Poseidon may have been mistaken, and it was not my chest to open. Instead, I continued to lie in bed, listening to the patterns of my heartbeat, and feeling the sly, unchanging breaths when I inhaled and exhaled.

This is ridiculous. I should just open it.

So I got up and sat on the edge of the bed. I rested my head in my hands, still hesitating. I shook my head and stood up, finally deciding to walk across the room. I grabbed the chest and sank back down on the bed.

The chest was heavy in my hands. Once more, I admired the strange tree etched on the bronze locks, feeling it on my fingertips. My heartbeat quickened, pounding faster and harder. My breaths became quick and shallow. My chest was tight, and my head was pounding, really hard, and starting to ache. The pounding in my chest got even harder. I put my hand over it as if to hold my heart back from pounding out. Suddenly, my chest felt like it broke open. I let out a groan, and then a yell. I held my hand tightly against it, but could see beams of light, actual light, shining through my shirt and fingers.

"What the hell?!" I cried. The light swallowed the sound of my yell, and me, and propelled me through it.

I saw the sailboat tied to the dock. The hooded woman and I were running in the sand. I was trailing behind her as she ran toward the shoreline. I watched in slow motion as her hood fell to her shoulders, letting her golden hair fall out to dance with the sunlight. I was no longer a little girl, but grown just as she was. I could hear her laughing and feel the warmth it gave me. I breathed in the scent of salt from the sea. It was windy, very windy, and her hair flew wildly, as did her white tunic. She laughed loudly as she began to turn around to face me.

My phone buzzed, the vibration closed my mind and vision, and I was back in my room, holding the old chest's lock. I had the sense I already knew who it was. I gulped the last breath I didn't know I was holding. My hand was still on my chest, which still felt open. I was so open, exposed, and aching. Finally, I reached over and picked up my phone.

I stared at the message. It had been a long time for her to text me all of a sudden. A month and six days exactly.

Are you awake?

My stomach dropped. The hand that was holding my chest fell to my stomach as if to make sure it was still there. All the while, my mouth began to dry up too quickly for my tongue to react. Taylor had messaged me, finally. My fingers felt fragile, like my open chest. I pressed each button carefully.

Yeah.

I waited for my phone to vibrate again. And waited. And waited. My eyes closed and I sighed. She was the oddest mortal I had ever met, and yet she had my body reacting just from the sound of her name or a single text.

I dropped the phone on the pillow along with my head. As my temple hit the soft cotton, I could not help but want to cry from all the senseless emotions I had for her.

Forget her. Just forget her.

∞

Troy eyed me from across the pool as he talked to Connor. He started taking off his shirt, his eyes still on me, making sure I was watching him. I couldn't help it. The term applied: his body *was* that of a Greek God.

He jumped in the pool and swam toward me. I sinfully watched him as he pulled himself onto the ledge, letting the water drip over his perfect, immortal body. One of the drops guided my eyes sensuously around his pecs and down his finely sculpted abs. He whipped his hair back and forth and then combed it back with his fingers. He smiled at me once he saw he'd caught my attention.

This time I didn't pull my eyes away.

He kept his smile on me the closer he walked and then paused before speaking. I thought it was for one final showcase before I moved my eyes up to his mouth. I could almost hear him say, "Yeah, look at me a little longer," which made me want to roll my eyes.

"Hey Troy." My voice came out annoyed.

He dropped his smile, grabbed the towel near my post, and draped it around his neck. "Hey, Petra, how's work today?"

"No one has drowned yet," I quipped. "So, good, I guess."

He laughed, and I stared blankly through him. He stared back at me, making certain he had heard my tone correctly. I tried to seem agitated, bothered that he was standing in my presence, but it was him who was too beautiful to be standing next to. He had perfectly toned and proportioned muscles. And his skin was tan, really tan—a shade of dark olive that made his white teeth and blue eyes shine even brighter.

"I just wanted to see how you're doing after the…" He paused. "You know, car accident?"

"Oh." I had forgotten he was even there. "I'm fine. … Thank you. It took a bit, but I healed right up."

His expression changed, and when it did, I felt his wariness. "Good. That's good."

He turned around to dive back in the pool, and I collapsed in the chair behind me with a gasp.

What is wrong with me? Why am I being so short with him?

Allison came around the pool. She waved and then greeted Connor and Troy before coming to my post. Since she'd come back from her trial with the Moirai, she'd been more social toward the other crewmembers, especially Troy. Although her smiles misled others, they did not fool me. I felt her more clearly than ever. She still missed her love. She reached my post, feeling discouraged.

"Is something wrong?" I asked.

She let out a sigh. "Taylor and I are having a hard time finding a place to live."

I had forgotten all about that. Was it fate that they needed a place now, just when we need roommates?

"Well the Gods may have answered you," I told her. "As of yesterday, Jaden and I have two rooms free."

Her eyes lit up. She popped up from her chair and grabbed me. "What? That's great!" She smiled.

"Come by tonight and we can talk to Jaden about it."

I gazed back out at the pool and caught Troy's eye. He nodded to me, as if beckoning me to come in. I shook my head and gave him a look like he was crazy.

"Come on. Live a little!" he shouted.

"I don't have my bathing suit on!"

He waded closer to the edge of the pool and gave me a look like I was the crazy one. "But you're the lifeguard." He chuckled. "You're supposed to be wearing one."

"Not really."

He laughed again. "Come on, get in the water."

"I'm allergic!" I yelled.

"You're bluffing!"

I smiled, and then turned around to Allison. She looked up from her phone. "I have to run, but I'll see you tonight? This will be great!"

I couldn't help but smile. *She's right. It's going to be fun living with them.*

But my smile slowly started to fade as I thought about Taylor—the girl who had started this. The mortal girl who'd broken a Goddess, who'd opened her chest to feel. The one I was supposed to be forgetting in order to mend—in order to help my kind.

∞

My mind was full of oppressive questions, all relating to Taylor and trying to forget. In actuality, I was thinking of her more than ever. I couldn't even hear Allison and Jaden speaking to me. I couldn't hear the television going in the background. I couldn't hear life playing around me anymore. How could I? My inner voice was louder. Why did I think about her so damn much? And why had I invited her to move in?

Allison walked into the kitchen with Jaden and started opening cabinet doors while asking rent questions. Apparently satisfied with her inspection, she announced that she was going to try calling Taylor again. I was sitting on the couch, trying to anticipate Taylor's answer as Allison dialed her number.

I could hear the ringing from the receiver, and then her voice. Her sudden, compelling, "Hello," made me choke on the breath I'd inhaled. It hit my eardrums, and a sudden rush of warmth came over my body like a torrent. I couldn't help but let the smile conquer my lips. I tried to tune in to every word. It had been too long since I'd heard her voice, and my reaction told it all.

Shit. I'm in trouble.

I caught wind of Allison's shock. Her body tensed up and her brow furrowed. "What? What are you talking about, Tay?" she asked softly.

She left the living room and went down the hall into another room. I started to get up and follow her but caught myself. Instead, my mind focused on Allison's emotions. She was confused. And then upset. Then agitated—furious almost. What was going on? My body became rigid. The sweet warmth of hearing Taylor's voice quickly left when I felt Allison's final emotion: defeated. Confusion flooded me. Taylor had said no. I knew it in my gut.

"Okay, fine, Tay. I understand," Allison said as she walked back into the living room. But she did not understand, not even in the slightest.

"What did she say?" I choked out. My mouth had gone dry.

"She said no. She found another place already."

"What?" Jaden replied, taking the words right from my mouth.

"What's wrong with her?" I asked.

"I don't know," Allison said. "She sounded strange. Something wasn't right."

"Well, at least she told us sooner than later," Jaden said with a shrug. "I'm still down for you to live here."

Allison sighed. "Yeah..." She paused and then her gaze met mine. I felt her heartbeat quicken, as did mine. Then she smiled. "Yeah... I'm in."

"Well alright!" Jaden said excitedly. "You can start moving in whenever you want."

I tried smiling at them. I tried to feel happy at everything that had just happened. But who was I kidding? My excitement had ended when that phone call did. She'd lied, and I knew the reason for that lie. The answer was clear: Taylor didn't want to move in because of me.

Chapter 9

Aphrodite's Account

It was done. We'd had the contract drawn up and signed. After Allison left to start her packing, I looked at Jaden and, without saying a word, ran to my bedroom before she could witness my breakdown. I lay down on my pillow and let it soak up every tear, overwhelmed by the feeling of wanting my mother. Growing up I had watched her lend her shoulder whenever my siblings' tears were flowing. In those days I'd never needed her, and yet I needed her now. I needed love now.

I lifted my swollen eyes from the pillow and spotted the chest across the room. I had a strange fascination with it, as if it was calling for me, and I wanted to hurry up and open it to see what it was it wanted. I got out of bed, grabbed it, and sat back down. I held it in my lap as I weighed out what could possibly be in it. And again, I gazed at the tree engraved on the locks. My fingers grazed it once more. This time no vision of the woman came, or anything else for that matter.

On each side of the bronze locks, keyholes were fastened below the engraved trees. It looked like an old skeleton key would unlock them. I assumed Poseidon had it and didn't think to give it to me. I fiddled with both locks for a good while until finally I gave up and threw the chest across the room. It hit the wall with a thud and fell to the ground, where it tumbled into the corner.

A light suddenly breached my bedroom window. I thought it was the full moon until I realized the glow belonged to a dove as white as snow sitting on my windowsill. For a quick second, I thought how strange it was for a dove to be here at this time of the night, but then shook the thought from my mind. Of course this was no ordinary dove.

It flew up and around me before descending and then transforming into my beautiful best friend, Apria. I was a bit surprised to see her in my room, but not really at the same time. I had known she would probably be checking up on me every now and again to see how my mending was going.

My eyes followed her as she came and sat next to me on my bed.

"Your timing is impeccable," I said.

She smiled. "How is mending?" she asked lightly.

My body slumped, recalling what I was doing only minutes before she came. I had not mended, not after my car accident, not even after I'd received ambrosia. There was no indication at all that my open chest was closing. I had too many things to say to her, to ask her, but wordless breaths were all I could manage.

"Tell me what you need from me?" she finally said, seeing the discouragement in my eyes.

"Truth," I said. "Truth is all I need."

She eyed me carefully without speaking, and then finally nodded. Still, there was doubt.

Afraid of what her answer would be, I hesitated, but I needed to know. "Am I a Nurtured?"

Her head lifted as if I had disgraced her somehow. She was angry with me then, though she did not allow it to show. She gracefully stood and walked across the bedroom, then stopped at my desk and stared as if she were seeing the landscape beyond. I felt her in a trance, her mind somewhere far, not here, not in the present moment.

"Why couldn't you tell me?" I asked.

She turned around quickly and what my eyes beheld was nothing I had ever expected. She began to cry, and her tears expressed what her lips couldn't say. She swiftly came to me and swallowed my body in her arms. As she tightly hugged me, I felt every bit of sadness in her now in me. A tear fell from my eye, and more quickly followed.

"I couldn't let you get hurt," she said softly.

Hurt? Hurt from what?

There was a second where my mind doubted we were speaking of the same thing. She pulled back and held me out in front of her, and then reached to wipe away my tears, but her tender touch only made more fall. She reached toward me once more, but then time stopped again.

Sand was everywhere, on my body and beneath my knees. The smell of the sea stung my eyes, which made me cry anew. My lips were dry, blistered and stinging from the salty tears. Apria held me in her arms still, but they were tight, as if to keep me from doing something. I was holding something in my hand. A dagger. The vision blurred as more tears fell from my eyes.

"Aphrodite, why! Aphrodite, end it," I begged. "Please, Aphrodite, end it all."

It had come in a flash but felt longer. We were back in my bedroom, but the vision was still as real as Apria's hands touching me now.

"Aphrodite, end it," I whispered. My own voice echoed in my head with the most painful sadness. I realized Apria was looking at me with shock; her hands gripped my shoulders tightly. Had she seen it too? Had we travelled in time? Or was it a premonition?

Both our eyes were wide, as if we were choking one another with our stares.

"Di-did you see it too?" I asked.

Her hands were shaking. We both looked at them, and she quickly pushed away from me. She was frightened. We both were.

"Se-see what?"

"See us. We were crying," I gasped. "I was holding a dagger."

She put a finger to my mouth to shush me. "You saw no such thing," she said. Her words were ice, but I felt her anger and fear beneath the cold.

"What?" I asked, unyieldingly. "What's there to hide?"

"I say stop," she ordered calmly.

I recoiled, terrified of incurring her wrath. She turned around, back to my desk, and her eyes caught on something.

"Where did you get this?" she asked angrily.

I saw where her eyes had landed: in the corner of my bedroom, on the rustic chest. Before I could answer, I sensed her more enraged than before. Suddenly, I realized I didn't need to fear her anger toward me; it was her knowledge of the chest that made her so angry.

"It was given to me," I said curtly.

She disliked my answer very much. Her lips pinched together, and she spoke through gritted teeth. "I am no adversary of yours, Petra."

"Then do not speak to me as if I am yours!" My voice began to rise. "You're dishonoring our friendship with hidden truths, Apria! I can feel you!"

My angry words hushed her. She did not say anything more.

Then I felt Jaden coming down the hall. My bedroom door swung open suddenly, slamming into the wall. Jaden stood in the doorway and glared at my contender. Her brow released its ferocious furrow once she saw who it was, and then immediately she sank into a kneel.

"O', I'm sorry, my lady," she said. "I did not know Petra had a guest over."

75

My lady? Jaden spoke to Apria like she was an Elder. I almost laughed at her mistake. Apria and I released our ardent stares at one another and regained our composure.

"It's quite alright, dear," Apria said, finally shifting her eyes to Jaden. "I don't think we've met." She glided over and stuck her hand out.

Jaden approached Apria with more discretion than I had ever seen anyone display. It felt like it took forever before they finally shook hands.

"Jaden. Jaden Krowe," she said, staring up into Apria's sapphire eyes.

In that moment, I wondered who was more enchanting, a blood relative of Aphrodite or a Nymphet of Poseidon. They held the handshake for a while, as if their hands were having words as well, until finally Jaden pulled away.

"Well, I'll leave you two alone," Jaden said.

Before she turned, Apria held out an arm out and stopped her. "No. I'm leaving anyway."

She gave me a pointed yet gentle look, and took one last look at the chest before spinning around, turning herself back into the beautiful white dove, and then flying out the window into the dark sky.

"What did she want with you?" Jaden asked, still staring out the window. I felt her nerves trembling.

"I don't quite know," I said softly, asking myself the same question. "Though I sensed her interest in my chest was a bit eerie."

Jaden kept staring out the window, her face as white as the dove Apria had turned into.

"Is something the matter?" I asked.

"I can't believe this," she muttered.

"What?"

"The young ones never see her."

She was talking to herself, though she said it loud enough for me to hear.

"See who?" I asked.

"Her," she said, pointing a finger out the window. "Aphrodite!"

I didn't meant to laugh in her face, truly, and I meant to apologize, but it all came rolling out.

"That's not Aphrodite, Jaden," I said finally between laughs. "That's my best friend, Apria Doves."

Her serious stare changed into a sure expression. Her emotions hit my skin, instantly halting my laughter.

"No, Petra," she said sternly. "That's Aphrodite."

∞

Without telling me where we were going, Jaden had Nick pick us up, and we began to fly southeast toward Texas. What would have been a day trip on land took us an hour in the sky. Jaden asked us to wear all black, so I could only assume we were going somewhere I should remain unseen—the Heavens.

It was dark when we landed, almost midnight. I knew exactly where we were. Ahead, about half a mile away, was the gargantuan front door of the deserted Gaianus School for Gods and Goddesses. We did not take the marble staircase to the front doors, but instead went around the back of the granite and marble columns to the side of the school. Not a single deity was present, for the school was no longer open.

Jaden stopped suddenly, kneeling behind some of the earthworks. She waited for Nick and me to do the same.

"Why am I here again?" Nick whispered.

"Shush!" she told him. "You said you wanted to help."

She crawled a couple of steps forward until she hit something with her open fist. Nothing happened, so she hit it again, this time harder, and then a few times more in a rhythmic sound. Whatever she was hitting finally budged. She crawled into the opening and disappeared into the darkness. Nick and I waited for a bit until suddenly she reappeared.

"What are you guys doing?" she asked in a loud whisper. "Follow me."

She disappeared into the darkness once more, and this time we followed. We reappeared on the other side and before us was a library larger than any I had ever seen before. I first thought we had gone underground at Gaianus or into another room, but we must have gone through a portal because the library spread out farther than the main building.

Everywhere, tall cases reached into the Heavens, filled with thousands upon thousands of books, templates, and scrolls. Archaic statues of different cultural Gods stood tall in front of every row on both sides of the long aisles in front of us. I looked back expecting to see a door, but there were only two marble columns and a slab reading, *'The place of the cure of the soul.'* Even more extraordinary, past the columns and down a trail was the most beautiful and luxurious garden.

"Isn't it great?" Jaden asked.

My eyes were still taking it all in. It was more than just great. It was miraculous.

"Where are we?" I asked.

"The Library of Alexandria."

"Didn't it burn down?"

"No," she said, giggling.

"It was moved," Nick said. "That was just a lie told to the mortals."

And to Gaianus students. I shook my head.

"How does someone move all…" I gestured to the mountains of bookcases, "this?"

"The same way we've just come," Jaden said.

"Teleportation!"

She nodded, smiling.

My head ran in circles. More than anything, I wanted to explore, but my mind's questions paralyzed me. I was in the Library of Alexandria, holding all the answers to Earth's questions. I had to laugh at the thought that I had teleported to the Heavens more times in the past 72 hours while banished than I had in a whole summer time when I was free. I had never broken any of Zeus' laws before, and now here I was breaking several.

"Come," Jaden said. "Let me show you the reason we're here."

How she found what she needed baffled me. Hanging from a ladder as tall as a giant, she dropped a book into Nick's hands.

"I didn't know we had so much history to fill such a grand library," I said breathlessly, still looking around me. The walls seemed to be expanding, adding more and more bookshelves every time I looked.

Jaden slid down the ladder, and when she landed near my feet, she gawked at me. Nick burst into laughter.

She smiled. "It's not just *our* history, but others' as well." She patted my shoulder. "We aren't the only ones from the stars."

I shuddered as my mind suddenly expanded. A black tunnel appeared in my mind's eye and suddenly it became wide enough for me to see space, and beings of all kinds coming from different corners of the galaxy.

Jaden beckoned us to follow her as she took the oversized book from Nick's hands and slammed it on the table.

"Aphrodite's account," she said.

"Every deity has a book of their account," Nick said. "How and when we were created, our ancestry, the great or not so great things we have done, who we mated with or married, and where we last resided."

"Every one of us has one of these?" I asked.

"Every. Single. One," Jaden said, a bit too dramatically. "Only no one is allowed to see the accounts still being written." She looked at the book and reached to lift the cover. It opened, and she stared. "Huh, that's odd."

"What is?" I asked.

"When an account is still being written, the book doesn't open. It's as if it's glued shut," Nick explained.

"Ha!" Jaden shouted. "Just as I suspected!" She pointed and then beckoned me over. I looked where her finger was pointing. In the groove of the spine, I could see the remnants of pages that had been ripped from the book.

Nick grabbed the book and stared with his mouth wide open. "I have never seen such a thing." He closed the book and looked at the cover, pondering. "Jaden, why did you want to see Aphrodite's account? Is she still among the young?"

Jaden nodded. "Very much so. I saw her today with Petra."

Nick slammed the book down on the table. "O' balls of Uranus! What is she like? Is her beauty really mesmerizing?"

They sounded mad to my ears. Certainly, they could not be talking about Apria, the same young Goddess I had known my whole life.

"How do you know it's her, Jaden?" I asked, "Wouldn't other deities have realized it was her as well? I've known her all my life and no one has ever mentioned to me that she was the real Aphrodite."

Jaden stared at me. "Maybe in Zeus' kingdom, the young weren't given the right drawing of her."

I had a hard time believing her theory. Surely all the young immortals had learned the *same* scriptures and seen the *same* pictures. Suddenly, a small feeling of doubt began to surface within me. *Maybe she's right.* Quickly after that, I began feeling weak. Thankfully, a chair found me before my knees gave out. My head felt heavy.

"She comes from Aphrodite's bloodline," I said conclusively—stubbornly. "She's not *the* Aphrodite." I paused. "And if you really are convinced, then we should look for Apria's account."

They both stared at me for a while.

"There isn't an account for Apria," Jaden said finally.

She left the table and disappeared down an aisle. After a few minutes, she reappeared with another book in her hand. She set it on the table and began flipping through the pages. When she found the one she wanted, she stopped, turned the book around, and slid it across the table to me.

On the page was a colored sketch of the twelve Olympian Gods and Goddesses, all in their century-old attire and smiling at one another as if they didn't know the photo was being drawn. I spotted Aphrodite to the right, standing near Hephaestus. The first thing I noticed was her eyes: big and almond shaped, brightly glowing sapphire. Then her high cheekbones, round and blush. Her lips were plump and perfect, her skin bronzed as if kissed by Helios, the Sun God. She looked exactly like Apria did now.

As if my spirit had lifted from my body, I saw myself sitting while Jaden and Nick stared at me, waiting for me to speak. My spirit waited too. I saw my face reflected in my spirit's eyes, blank and pale. Slowly, my spirit reentered my body.

"I had a premonition of us," I muttered, and felt their confusion.

"Well?" Jaden nodded. "Go on. Tell us. What was it?"

"Today," I said, "before you came in my room and saw us talking, I was crying. Apria was comforting me. As she started wiping away my tears, my mind jumped as if we traveled in time. All of a sudden, we were on a beach on a small island. I had a dagger in my hand, and I cried out to her."

I felt their growing terror and wondered if I should stop. However, I was just as curious as they were and thought maybe they could decipher this in some way I could not.

"And in this premonition," I continued, "Apria, or Aphrodite, was securing me... consoling me. I cried out in the vision, 'Aphrodite, end it, end it all.' Then I came to and found Apria in front of me, back in my bedroom."

A few seconds passed before anyone said anything. None of it made sense. Could it have been just another dream?

"Is this the first time you've had one of these?" Jaden finally asked.

I shook my head. "I had a couple before, but this one was the first of Apria."

Jaden hopped onto the table. "Okay. Tell us every single one."

So I did. I started with the very first dream I'd had of the young woman wearing the hooded tunic. How I was young when she found me and spoke to me. I told them I could only see her eyes glowing out from the darkened hood. I was young to be alone, but I didn't know what had happened to my parents—I thought they must have been dead.

Then I told them of the dream I'd had while in the coma after the car hit me. In that dream, I was the same age as the young woman, and we were crying together. I told them how I'd felt her and my own pain so vividly. I decided to leave out that she'd kissed me, but told them she was saying goodbye for what felt like a very long time.

Finally, I told them of the flash of white I'd had while touching the lock on the chest. The same young woman and I were running on the beach, both the same age again, and a heavy wind knocked the woman's hood off and unveiled her golden hair.

"Your senses worked?" Jaden asked.

"Yes," I said. "I smelled the salt of the sea and could feel the sand beneath my knees, and the wind's salty breeze… everything as if it were real. As you and I are here right now."

"Did you look the same as you do now? Like, your body was the same body and your hair was the same color?"

"No," I said, and began to think. "No, my skin was olive. Not pale like mine. And I wasn't tall and slender but a little shorter and muscular." I paused. "I'm completely different in the dreams."

"It was no dream," Jaden said. "I believe those moments happened."

Nick and Jaden shared glances.

"They must be memories from a past life," she said softly.

I gulped. Suddenly, I wanted to give up. I was not ready for this. I felt the need to run far away from the secrets before more began to unveil themselves. I must have looked weak, pale, like I was out of my wits. I sure as hell felt like I was!

Jaden eyed Nick for a second. It reminded me of what Apria and Dion used to do before telling me something important. Had Apria and Dion known these secrets all along? Had they tried to tell me when we were in the Underworld standing in the white room?

I tried hard to remember what had happened then.

"Lethe," I whispered.

"What was that?" Nick asked.

"In the Underworld," I recalled. "Something happened when we went to rescue John from Hades." I gulped. "I crossed Lethe, but Apria and Dion crossed Acheron." I shook my head. Remembering it now, I could almost feel the gray, grotesque creatures' nails scratching my skin. "It made no sense to me then. And Dion and Apria said I must have been brought to Lethe by Hades for a reason… to finish the process of my incarceration—"

"That makes sense," Jaden said under her breath.

"What?" Nick and I asked simultaneously.

"It's reincarnation, not incarceration," she said. "I don't know why they told you that."

"Reincarnation?" I asked.

"Yes! To finish the process of your *reincarnation*."

She felt more excited than I was. Another secret revealed, and I was still catching up with the first one.

"This all makes sense," she repeated. "That's why you're having those visions. Your process wasn't finished. Therefore, you're remembering your past life." She brought her finger to her chin, thinking. "But how could one's process not get finished? Hades gives enough to drink from Lethe for the moral mortal not to remember their new life…"

She was speaking more to herself than to me, and I waited for her to think it out, my mind still too heavy to try.

"Unless," she said finally, now speaking directly to me. "Hades wanted you to remember something. Or," she shouted, getting even more excited, "Hades wasn't the one who brought you to Lethe!"

"Then who?" Nick took the question right from my tongue.

Jaden didn't answer right away. She was still thinking.

"Reincarnated," I said softly. In that moment, I began to understand. "Nurtured," I mumbled.

"Do you think it was the woman in your visions who did this?" Nick asked.

"Do you know her?" Jaden asked.

"No." I shrugged and then paused. "But maybe the chest Poseidon gave me has the answers to who she was. Do you think that's why Apr– Aphrodite was so interested in it?"

"Could be," Jaden answered. "Could be for other reasons too. … We need to look into it and find out."

"We can't," I said, discouraged. "I don't have the key."

A smile began to grow on her face. "Then let's go find it!"

Chapter 10

Poseidon's Kingdom

I could have stayed in the library of Alexandria forever if Jaden had let me. But she took me home and put me to bed and told me to rest, for tomorrow I was going to need all my strength. For what exactly, I was not sure.

I dreamt of her again that night, the hooded young woman with eyes like the sea. I was young this time, no more than a teen. It was night, and she was still wearing her hood as we sat by a low campfire. I held a papyrus scroll in one hand and in the other a charcoal stick to write with. Her face was just as dark as ever, but her eyes reflected the campfire's flames, looking like more of a purplish blue. She kept pointing to the night sky, teaching me of the stars, of each constellation and their meaning. My writing was horrendous. She saw my struggle and came around the fire, reached for my hand to help me write. I squinted at her face through the darkness, trying to see if I could get a glimpse of her lips.

"Petra," she whispered. "Petra wake up!"

I opened my eyes and saw Jaden standing over me. I quickly sat up in bed. Nick and Ricky were standing in the shadows of my bedroom. I was delighted to see them, to know they wanted to take this journey with me, wherever it was we were going.

Nick stepped out of the shadows with a big smile. "Let's go find this key."

We drove west with the sun rising on our backs; I imagined three bodies would have been too much for Nick to carry as he flew. It was a long drive, and we sat in silence for hours, staring out the windows, deep in our own thoughts. I could not get my dream out of my head. I was still having a hard time coming to terms with the idea that these dreams were possibly not dreams at all, but visions from my past life. Out of the many questions I had, one of them was on replay this morning: Why was I young in some visions and grown in others, while the hooded woman always looked the same age? The thought kept eating away at my brain, until finally I decided I needed a second opinion.

"I had another vision," I blurted, breaking hours of silence.

Jaden, who was driving, swung around her seat, making the car swerve. "What?"

Nick, who sat in the passenger seat, swung around to look at me as well. "What was it this time?"

Ricky, whom I assumed Nick had told everything, sat quiet but wide-eyed in the seat next to me.

I gulped.

"Well, let's hear it!" Nick said, excitement twinkling in his eyes.

I sighed. "I was a teenager, I think. The hooded woman was sitting with me. It was dark and we had a small fire burning. I have yet to see her face. I was writing something, and she kept pointing to the stars. I think she was teaching me about them, as well as teaching me how to write. When I couldn't write well, she helped me. That's it. Then Jaden woke me up."

"Damnit, Jaden," Nick shouted.

"What?!" she yelled back.

"Why do you think I keep changing age in these visions?" I asked, interrupting their quarrel.

"Well that should be an easy answer," Ricky said. I had almost forgotten he was there.

I looked at him, hoping he would just say it. If it was true, I needed to hear it out loud and not have it stuck in my head. My brain was fried already.

"You *were* still growing," he said. "Depending on the timeframe, you may have been mortal. Where she clearly was not."

I let out a breath of gratitude. "That explains it…"

When immortals are born, we grow at an exponential rate, about five or six times faster than mortals. Then, when we get to be twenty, we slow way down, to nearly ten times slower than mortals.

"Each vision was not only a different time in the past, but my feelings for her were different, from when I was young to when I was mature. I admired her terribly when I was a child, yet I was deeply in love with her when we were the same age."

"It seems she took you in as a child," Ricky said, "and became your lover when you grew older."

"A Lambda in your past life too," Nick muttered.

"What?" Jaden asked. I saw her hurt expression in the rearview mirror and let my head fall into my hands.

"Uh—" Nick stuttered.

"What do you mean?" Jaden asked.

I lunged across the seat toward her. "Jaden, I've been wanting to—"

She swerved again, this time pulling off onto the side of the road. She stopped the car abruptly and then hopped out. I jumped out after her and followed her down a red dirt trail. She finally stopped and then knelt and started muttering. I stumbled up to her, and as I got closer, I realized she was praying. I let her finish, and before I could begin to explain, she stood up and turned around.

"It's Ashton!" she exclaimed.

How did she know about Ashton?

Sensing my confusion, she continued, "When she stayed the night this past spring… You just about threw up your breakfast telling me you guys had kissed."

I remembered the night Ashton had spent with me because Taylor had insisted she should sleep over. The memory of Ashton's touch on my chest and her lips on mine gave me a slight shiver. I recalled my paranoia the next morning, thinking Jaden knew we had kissed, only to find out she didn't care.

"That kiss meant something more? Do you love her?" she asked me now.

I couldn't speak. I wanted to tell her she was wrong; it wasn't Ashton's kiss that had me feeling my emotions, but Taylor's. However, I had not told her about the kiss Taylor and I had shared. Tears started to build in my eyes. I couldn't form her name on my lips. Speaking it felt like a crime. I held my eyes on the red dirt.

"No," I mumbled. "Not Ashton…" I finally lifted my eyes back up to Jaden, but still couldn't say her name. I could feel Jaden becoming impatient

"Well?"

I shook my head.

"Are you a Lambda or not?"

My head shook harder. "No, Jaden," I said softly. "I'm not a Lambda."

She watched me, questioning my words, and then let a small curve of a smile develop on her lips. "You should put more trust in me."

I looked away from her. I could feel her anger ceasing, but there was still hurt beneath her words. I wanted to ease her pain and tell her why I was embarrassed to tell her.

"I'm banished from the Heavens," I muttered softly, though hoping she still was able to hear me. The look on her face told me she did not. "I didn't decide to come back to Earth this summer," I said, speaking louder this time. "I had to."

She gave me a solemn expression and nodded her head. "So you *are* a Lambda."

I shook my head once again. "Before school ended, the Moirai saw I would become one. So I'm banished to await my trial." I stopped suddenly, fearing the truth I was about to speak held too much humiliation. I wasn't ready to disclose my duty to her, which was to forget Taylor and do away with my emotions.

My answer saddened her. I think she knew it, too. "I'm your guardian. You can tell me these things," she said finally. "You can trust me."

∞

California was a lot hotter than Colorado in the summer. The sun felt close to our heads as we stood on the rocky peak of the cliff, looking down at the roaring waves hitting the jagged rocks sticking out from the water. The memory surfaced once again of the time I'd stood on this cliff with my brother John. The memory of his tears shot through my bones; his beloved had broken his heart. He'd wanted his torture to end, and had asked Poseidon to be the one to end it.

Zeus's law says we cannot end a life, especially not our own. Only fate can. But the Elder Gods like Poseidon have the power to banish a God or Goddess to Tartarus or destroy their soul. My brother wanted the latter. I hated that memory more now that my feelings were alive. I quickly shook it from my head and came to, just in time to hear Jaden.

"See that rock," she said pointing down at the angry ocean below, "the tallest one peeking over the water?"

We all nodded. It was a very jagged rock with a cusped face, about a yard away from the cliff; if we were to fall, we would miss it.

"Jump as far as you can toward it," Jaden said with a smile. "Try to land on it."

"Nearly suicide for a mortal," Ricky said.

Her smile grew wider. "Well thankfully, we aren't that."

I swallowed hard. *Barely.*

I stood on a large rock to get my footing. Ricky and Nick followed suit, standing next to me. We eyed each other as if counting down.

"Wait!" Jaden shouted before we bent down to jump. "We have to wait a couple of minutes for it to be 11:11. I timed it nearly perfect." She smiled.

"Why? So we can make a wish when we fall?" Nick snorted.

"No," she said, glaring at him. "That's when the gateway opens to Poseidon's Kingdom."

Nick shut his mouth, which made me laugh.

Jaden eyed her wristwatch carefully. "Okay, get ready." She paused. "Now!"

We leapt toward the jagged rock. It was a freefall unlike any other. Then my mind shot through time into another memory. I was older, and my body had started to develop as well as my penmanship. I chiseled away at the stick of charcoal, and then started writing on a scroll. I could barely make out the words, though the structure looked like a sonnet or a poem. A beautiful voice whispered in my ear, and I looked up into a pair of sapphire eyes.

With a huge splash, the cold ocean awoke me from my daydream. I gasped for breath, and to my surprise, drew one in even though I was under the sea. A hand grabbed mine and I looked over to see Jaden smiling at me. With her other hand, she beckoned Ricky and Nick to follow us as we swam deeper into the dark blue.

Two beautiful Nymphets soon appeared to greet us. I swam closer, and to my surprise, Diane was one of them. I was happy to see her, and we followed them until we came to a gigantic golden gate that reached endlessly up to the unseen surface and was several miles wide. The gates opened briskly.

We swam through, still following Diane and the other Nymphet. Once they passed the gates, their feet fell down, and they began to walk though there was no visible surface. Our feet, too, began to walk on the hidden surface. I looked below and marveled at what I saw. The surface we were standing on was the night sky, full of stars and planets, though not from Earth's solar system. It was as if we were walking in space. I looked at Jaden in disbelief, but all she did was smile.

We soon reached a staircase of green marble with gold accents leading to another golden gate, just as big as the first one. However, clouds surrounded this one.

"Are we under the sea, or in the Heavens?" Ricky asked.

"This is Poseidon's Kingdom," Jaden said with a gleaming smile. "This is *our* Heaven." She breathed in deeply. "Feels good to be home."

I imagined that if I were ever to see Zeus's temple, this was what it would look like. Nick, Ricky and I wore identical expressions, mouths wide and smiling and eyes twinkling at everything we saw around us. In that moment, I was convinced I saw perfection.

We reached the golden gate in the clouds and it slowly opened on a city—a beautiful, perfect city. Before me were beautiful lights and golden temples and dwellings where the Nymphets, mermaids, and sea creatures all lived. It was a kingdom unlike any I had ever seen before, and all of it lay over the night sky as if the city was floating in space.

In the farthest distance, on top of an immaculate emerald hill, sat Poseidon's temple. We were awed at the view as we started into the city. Huge, beautiful seahorses, whales, dolphins, and colorful breeds of gilled, winged horses flew all around us freely through the streets.

Every Nymphet, mermaid, and sea creature seemed to be in a rush, though each still took a second to welcome us or acknowledge us with absolute kindness. Many mermaids grew fond of Nick and Ricky and began to trail slightly behind them, giggling with shy smiles every time one of them turned around and waved.

As we made our way through the city and up the hill to Poseidon's temple, I grew wary thinking of what I would find inside the chest, if Poseidon gave me the key. However, the rush of excitement over finally meeting Poseidon tucked the thought in the back of my head. Every now and then Jaden would look over at me, either to make sure I was okay or to see if I was still there.

Diane finally stopped us in a gigantic hallway with green and gold pillars on each side. Beyond the pillars, it was open and gave a 360 view of the gold and emerald kingdom and its sparkling lights.

Diane turned around to face us. "Remember, the Elders fluently speak the old language. You will address Poseidon as *Kýrios*."

I must have been the only one who hadn't known that, for I was the only one who nodded my head. Immediately after Diane said this, I heard my name being called. It was a beautiful, calming sound.

Suddenly, the great Poseidon himself was in front of my very own eyes. No dream overcame me this time, no vision… He was most certainly real. And huge! We knelt to honor him. I gazed at his feet and at the end of his great, glowing, golden trident. It was double the size of my body.

"Stand," he said, his voice calm.

We stood, and craning up as far as my neck could stretch, I got a good look at him. He was no less than thirteen feet tall with protruding muscles, resembling a rhinoceros. His beard of silver, gold, green, and brown braids reached his chest. His eyes were emerald and fierce as he stared at me with a perplexed expression.

"*Fef!*" he shouted. "You have a say about your chest?"

"I do, my *Kýrios*," I said. "I fear you have mistaken its owner."

He laughed a great laugh that made the temple tremble. "*Paidi mou,* no mistake. It is yours."

I looked at his great smile with curiosity and had to wonder what made him so confident in his answer.

"It is without a key, great *Kýrios*," Ricky said.

Poseidon eyed him intently, and then slowly reached for his chin, hidden beneath his thickly braided beard.

"*O' skatá!*" he shouted. "No key?" He laughed.

"We thought you might have it?" I said.

"*O' paidi mou*, no, not me," he said earnestly, touching his chest. He then folded his fingers until one was pointing at me. "*Thymámai…* Remember."

As that word gently left his lips, a great force hit me from behind. It lifted me out of the great hallway and into the reflective outer space. I tried to turn my head to look below me and caught a glimpse of a gigantic wave. I was on the face of the wave, riding it as it grew higher and higher. With one flick of the wave, my body was flung up and hung in the darkness of space. It felt like I was floating, just for a second, and within that second I reached out, thinking I could touch the stars or the sea's surface. Then the face of the wave came crashing down, and I along with it. The wave slammed me into the ground, knocking the wind out of me. I lay in the sand, choking out all the water that filled my lungs, then rolled over onto my hands and knees still coughing. I let out a breath and took another one in. The soft breeze carried the fresh scent of salt and seaweed. I wiped my soaking wet hair away from my face and eyes and scanned around me to see where I was. I wasn't in the temple anymore. In fact, I was far away from Poseidon's Kingdom, on an island.

My feet planted in the sand. I felt discouraged, not knowing if I was in my reality or not. The island felt strangely familiar. Was this the island of my dreams? Or was I having another vision?

The sun warmed my back. I lifted my head and kissed the sky with my eyes. I could feel the island call to my body, and my body benevolently respond. This island was home.

Voices began echoing not far from me. One spoke, and then another right after. I followed the sounds into the trees, toward where the brush met a small brook. In the brook two young Goddesses were bathing. My feet stopped when I saw them, and I quickly hid myself downstream behind a boulder twice my size. They spoke again, their voices fluent and beautiful with the old language. I didn't have a clue what they were saying, but one Goddess' tone sounded teasing and playful and the other's shy. I edged around the rock, eager to get a better look at their glowing faces, staying low to the ground.

Finally, I saw the Goddess closest to me. Her back was facing me so I could not get a good look at her, but she had golden, sun-kissed hair adorned with a beautiful flower wreath. I looked up and saw the other Goddess facing her, smiling. Her hair was dark like the night, and her eyes a piercing blue that resembled Ashton's. She started speaking as she flicked stream water at the other Goddess.

The sun peeked from around the trees and shed its beam on the water where they were standing, now bathing in its rays. Just as that happened, the Gods granted me understanding of their ancient tongue, and I began to hear the words they spoke.

"O' beloved," the dark-haired Goddess said. "She is not so awful."

"She can be frightening at times. Do you agree to that at least?" the golden-haired Goddess asked.

The dark-haired Goddess crossed her arms and poked at her chin. "She is passionate, which can make her frightening. But you cannot fault her," she told the other as she waded closer. "She is my sister, for the Gods' sake. She would not deny anyone of whom I am so fond."

The golden-haired Goddess's back was still toward me, but I could imagine the comment made her blush. The dark-haired Goddess closed in on her and put something around her neck. She must have liked it, for she jumped into the dark-haired Goddess's arms and they embraced each other in a passionate kiss.

Quickly, they began to undress each other. The half-sheer garments they wore fell around them and slowly drifted down the stream. One caught on a rock, but the other drifted to my side and I saw it was a white hooded garment.

There was no letting up on their fire. I closed my eyes to give them privacy. Was this what Poseidon willed me to witness? Thinking there was nothing else I should see, I started crawling away from the rock.

"Peitho," I heard. "Peitho, but Peitho…"

I turned back around. That name… Where had I heard that name before? The golden-haired Goddess, whose back was still to me, pulled away from the dark-haired Goddess called Peitho and held her at arm's length.

"I am still wary of her," the golden-haired Goddess said. "She is very powerful, and if she were to know…"

"She won't know," Peitho said. "She can't find us here. This island is sacred. It is on no map the Olympians know, for it is endlessly buoyant… Just like my love for you."

I imagined the golden-haired Goddess must have blushed again. Peitho smiled a beautiful, innocent smile.

"Yes," the golden-haired Goddess said. "Let us bless the island, Petra." She leaned in and claimed Peitho's lips with her own.

My knees gave way and I fell into the stream. They must have spotted me, and they knew who I was. Quickly, I stood and scrambled behind the boulder, only to find they were still engrossed in each other's lips.

They must have not meant me; I guess the island's name is Petra?

As they stood bare, wading in the water, holding one another as though they hadn't seen each other in decades, I felt a sudden ache in my chest, the kind of ache I got only when thinking of Taylor. I missed her as I watched these Goddesses passionately embrace one another in this dream—if it was a dream. Suddenly, I felt sick to my stomach.

Peitho spun the golden-haired Goddess around and laid her out over the bank of the brook, even closer to where I stood behind the giant boulder.

The golden-haired Goddess leaned up slightly and whispered, "I love you, my Peitho."

Peitho looked at the golden-haired Goddess for a very long time until finally, and ever so softly, she said, "I will love you forever—"

I slipped on a small rock and fell forward in full view of them, only a couple of feet from where they lay on the bank. But they did not stop nor ease up. They didn't even lift their eyes in my direction. As I stood before them, I thought they would notice me, but still neither of them flinched. I was invisible to them.

As their kisses drove out more passion, I became aware of the possibility that I was not in their reality and therefore they could not see me. Without knowing why, my tears began to build. I moved away from the lovers and raised my head once again to the sky.

Why does this make me so sad?

I shook my head and let my gaze drift. Then something caught my eye. Past the lovers, in a brush of green where wild myrtle grew, someone else was hiding—someone with glowing sapphire eyes.

My hand grabbed my mouth, tucking the gasp back deep in my throat. It was Aphrodite. And she looked pissed.

∞

I awoke in my bed back home in Colorado, sweating and panting as if I'd just run a few miles.

A dream. It was only a dream. I tried to calm myself. But it was Apria. It was Aphrodite. She was everywhere. Why?

I had to find out. Was there ever a floating island called Petra? Most importantly, why had Poseidon dropped me there?

For the first time, I took hold of my chest and grieved over my heart. I wished for a love like theirs, like Peitho and the golden-haired Goddess. I wanted to feel the love they'd shared on the bank of the brook with the young hooded woman I saw in my dreams. Not Taylor, surprisingly. No, I wished for the hooded woman, not in a past life, not in my dreams, but now, in my current life. Peitho and the golden-haired Goddess had shown me that such a beautiful love could exist.

Peitho? Who is Peitho?

Chapter 11

Truths and Dares

My eyes hung on the minute hand as the clock finally hit 5:01. I glared out at the pool; there wasn't a single person in it. But I kept sitting at my post as if waiting for something, someone—answers. I found myself gazing across the pool as the building lights grew fainter, until finally there were only the pool lights on in the building. Everything was even quieter without the buzzing of electricity from the fluorescent lights. I contemplated whether I liked it or not. It was a rarity for me to experience noiseless surroundings. I stared into the pool and imagined the brook and the two Goddesses. There was nothing peaceful about it. It felt like more of a yearning—a wanting.

Peitho, a Goddess I'd never seen before and had yet to remember where I'd heard her name, was a mystic in my mind. Someone I really wanted to know. Almost had to know. She had eerily similar features to Ashton, and while I didn't want to draw any conclusions, I was desperate for a lead on how I could find her. If she was even real.

I closed my eyes and felt a soft, solitary thump through my chest, in my ears and echoing through my body. My breaths became quieter and deeper. Everything from my past seemed unreal, and it was all because of Aphrodite. My best friend for all these years—had she falsified her true self to me? And for what? What was she hiding? Why could she not tell me she was the great Olympian Goddess of Love? Was it love to lie for more than a century of your life? Were the stories of her family and growing up all lies? Could I believe anything she said ever again?

I could feel it growing later and later, but I didn't want to go home. Allison had officially moved in. I knew I needed to tell Jaden, Ricky, and Nick about what Poseidon had shown me, but I needed more time to think about what I'd seen.

The pool door opened and slammed shut, the sound echoing off the still pool and throughout the building.

"Petra? What are you doing here?"

I knew that voice, so I kept my gaze on the pool and answered quietly. "Hey Troy, I'm—" I hesitated, thinking, "meditating."

I finally looked up, just in time to see him pull off his shirt. "They say water helps with meditation…"

I smiled back at him. "I'm sure."

He lightly laughed and then jumped into the pool. I watched him as he swam underwater toward me. His face broke the surface, followed by his whipping hair. He reached for the edge of the pool, only his fingertips holding the ledge, and gave me a playful grin.

"Well?" he said.

"Well what?"

"Work's over… I don't need a lifeguard." He paused. "Are you coming in or what?"

"No," I said without missing a beat.

He gave a sad attempt at a pout. "Why?"

"Because I really don't have a bathing suit on."

He waited for my solemn expression to change, to see if I was kidding, and then smiled. "But you're the lifeguard."

"I have never needed to save anyone. And I figure that if someone was drowning, I wouldn't care about diving in with clothes on to save them."

He gave a slight nod of agreement and chuckled. An awkward silence followed.

"Can I ask you a truth?" he asked suddenly.

I thought for a second and then nodded.

"Do I smell bad?"

"What? No."

"Oh," he pondered. "It seems you never want to be around me."

"That's not true."

"Okay," he smiled. He let go of the edge of the pool and started treading lightly, content with my answer. Then, following a new thought, he came back to the edge of the pool and looked up at me intriguingly. "Want to play a game?"

I laughed at him.

"Come on," he said. "Entertain me."

I looked at his eagerness as if it were a child's, which admittedly was a cute look on him. I nodded. "Sure."

"Let's play a game of truths and dares," he said.

"No."

His second attempt at pouting was better. "Why not?"

I didn't know why. I guess I wasn't in the mood for games. I shook my head and snapped, "Fine."

"Yes!" he shouted. "I dare you to jump in the pool."

I shook my head. "I believe it's my turn to ask you a truth."

His head popped up, and he asked in a strangely seductive voice, "Yeah?"

I hesitated at his demeanor. "Why do you care?"

"That you get in the pool?"

I gawked at him. "No, about me."

He let go of the ledge once again and started drifting away, stumped at my question. "I-I don't quite know. I just do. I seem to care a lot… about you."

I slumped. I had never even tried to reciprocate, and for that second, I felt awful about it. I should have been reciprocating, forgetting, mending. I should have been doing a lot of things other than what I had been doing. I looked up at the ceiling as if the Gods had cast this riddle upon me for their own entertainment.

"It's my dare now," Troy said, interrupting my thoughts.

"Okay. What?"

"I dare you to join me in the pool," he said charmingly.

"Couldn't have guessed it. You just don't let up, do you?"

He said nothing, only smiled so big it reached his eyes.

"Fine!" I said.

I stood up, took off my shirt, and threw it down beside the ladder to my post. I slowly and doubtfully slipped off my shorts and kicked them near my shirt. I could feel his eyes on me, watching carefully. His quickened heartbeat belied his apparent patience. I watched him try to hide his excitement. Feeling oddly comfortable, I let him see my bare body. I gave him a quick wink and smiled before diving from my post and into the pool.

The water crashed around my head, sliding down my body, and kissed my toes. An adrenalizing feeling overcame me, and my body relaxed. I let my body float under the water for a little longer, feeling the stress of everything wash away with the water's touch.

Why didn't I do this sooner?

My head broke through the surface for a fresh breath. I waited for the water to drip past my eyelids before opening them. When I did, Troy was staring at me with the most hopeful gaze. I couldn't help but think about how beautiful he looked in the lamplight.

"Thank you," he said.

"My dare now."

He laughed and gestured for me to speak.

"Let's make it fair, shall we?" I smiled, and then looked at his trunks.

His eyes questioned me, and then he laughed, thinking I was joking. "My shorts? But then I would be naked."

"It'd only be fair," I said.

He nodded and gave me a playful grin. "Okay then." He reached for his trunks, wiggling them off while keeping his flirty grin on me. His arm came up from under the water holding his shorts.

"Okay, they're off," he said, smiling, and then he threw them over the edge of the pool.

"Your turn," I said, nodding to him.

His smile grew bigger. "I dare you to kiss me for eight seconds."

"Wow, we're just going for it now, are we?" I laughed. He didn't reply, just kept smiling. "Eight seconds, huh?" I laughed again. "Why not round up?"

"I thought ten would be too long," he replied, still smiling.

I paused to feel him, to try and get a sense of exactly what it was he wanted. He was eager; I could feel his adrenaline pulsing through my ears. As I got closer to him, my smile slowly began to flatten. When I reached him, only one thought was screaming at me.

Will I feel love now?

My hands wrapped around the back of his neck, gently pulling him to me, pulling our bodies together. My chest and thighs brushed his. I looked into his eyes before reaching his lips and saw the compassion in them, and I smiled before leaning in.

Our lips met, and so did everything else. I felt his warmth crash into me. His whole body was excited, full of fire and desire. I couldn't help but push him toward the ledge. I felt my body wanting too, but it wasn't the same as Troy's want. My body didn't want to stop until I could feel the love Peitho and the Goddess had shared, but at the same time I wished to feel nothing at all.

His kiss was not soft, but hard and passionate. He didn't care to learn how our tongues worked together, didn't care to feel the structure of my lips and mouth.

97

Honestly, neither did I. I just wanted the pain to end. Our lips let go and I stared into his eyes. And felt nothing.

Has my chest finally mended?

I felt *his* spark of hope ignite within me. I did not welcome the thought so quickly, and so I pushed away from him, confused. I didn't feel anything from him. Was I beginning to mend, and was Troy the cure?

When he pushed back into me, I let him fall back onto my lips and gradually have his way with them. A flash of Taylor's face came into my mind and gave me a great and mortifying start, making me accidentally bite his lip and pull away again, hating that his hope had overtaken me. He must have thought the bite was on purpose and I was teasing, for he enjoyed it and pushed closer. I considered if I should press back or not, but then decided against it. I lifted my lips away from his once again. What was I doing?

I wanted this. I wanted the mending to stop. Didn't I? My head was splitting in two. I didn't know what I wanted at that moment. I didn't want my chest to close just yet. I felt as if I was betraying love. If my chest were to close, I would never experience the kind of love Peitho and the other Goddess had. Taylor's face popped into my mind once again. Why?

I dove back into his lips with even more fire than before. Troy reacted beautifully. He reached around my lower back, down to my bottom, and squeezed. In one swift movement, he picked me up and put me on the ledge. His fingers grasped my skin with such fire. I sensed exactly what he wanted with every touch. He was so easy.

This time, instead of fighting my chest opening, I embraced it, and him, and wrapped my legs around his back as I dove deeper into his mouth. His emotions now screamed even louder as the tips of his fingers moved over every inch of my body. He was excited, confused, getting what he wanted; all those feelings were in an uproar, vying with my own emotions. Taylor's face—our kiss, her lips—was all I could think about. Why?

I cannot. I can't.

And as I felt Taylor's lips, my lips pushed harder into Troy's. Taylor's touch came to me, her legs entwined with mine, her hands in my hair, her body clinging to mine. Her scent of lemongrass and pine.

Fuck.

I pulled away from Troy angrily. His body pushed forward. Pushing and pulling, our bodies were in a tangle, fighting and welcoming. I was confused. He was not. He dove in willingly, as my own chains of sin held me back.

What am I doing?

My hands moved from his neck and down his chest. I gave him one final, hard push, breaking our lips and bodies apart. We stared at each other for a couple of seconds. I was humiliated and angry at my thoughts, my actions.

I climbed out of the pool without saying a word, grabbed my clothes, and went out the door.

∞

I walked back home with the taste of him still on my lips and began to curse. *That was unlike me. What drove that out of me? Lust again?*

It could only be, for I had betrayed love and could not feel my heart anywhere, not even in the darkest corners of my body. Only lust was there, now the captain of my body. Fear and anger lay side by side within my open chest.

The stars were bright, and I stared at them the whole time, using them to guide me home instead of the streetlamps. Which one was I from? Which one would I awake and go home to? Was my home in the Heavens not really home? Were my dreams trying to show me where my true home was? Or were they just my subconscious yearning for a life I wished I'd lived? With that thought, warm tears begin to fall down my face, and I wiped them quickly away.

I opened the front door to the house thinking they would be sleeping or unpacking, but none of them were. Jaden and Allison were wide-awake. I sensed their excitement as soon as I entered the living room. Then the pop of a bottle. Champagne spilled over the floor along with their confusion when they saw me. I hadn't thought to look at myself in a mirror and could only imagine what I looked like—clothes half on, hair wet and tangled. They didn't understand, and I wouldn't know where to begin explaining. I ran to my room before they could see the tears fall. Only my pillow would see my tears tonight. I cried myself to sleep hoping to wake up from this dream. And maybe, just maybe, wake up in my hooded woman's arms.

Chapter 12

All for Love

I woke up to the gentlest touch on my chest. The scent of fresh jasmine and lavender skimmed my nose as hair tickled my face. A hand caressed my chest, and then, within a breath, she kissed me.

"I've missed you," she said.

My eyes opened with a smile, and the hooded woman from my dreams was leaning over me. I stared into her eyes as she leaned back in and gently kissed me again. The lips lifted from mine. With the moon lighting her face, I finally saw to whom the lips really belonged.

"Ashton?"

Was she real, or had I awakened into another dream?

She hushed me with a smile and whispered, "What a beautiful thing to come home to."

I dove into her arms. "Are you real?"

She nodded and kissed my brow. "I'm back from my judgment."

I let go of her warm hug and held her at arm's length. She really was here and not in Tartarus.

As if reading my thoughts, she said, "A second chance."

Joy, it must have been joy that filled my heart. I dove back into her arms. She kissed my brow and brought my chin up so our lips could meet. She began to lay me down gently, but I shoved her back.

"You can't be here," I whispered. I grabbed her arm and as quietly and quickly as I could, led her out the door and into the night.

We walked through the residential neighborhood and onto the Regis campus. Once I thought we were safe to talk above a whisper, I stopped.

"A lot has happened since you left," I told her.

She shook her head with a smile. "I can't imagine that. You look just as beautiful as when I left."

I blushed, and then sighed. "Allison lives with me now."

"I know," she said, still smiling.

"You do?"

"I do." She nodded. "I saw her car out front. I could only assume," she teased.

"And you still came in, knowing your very powerful ex-girlfriend is sleeping only a door down from me?"

She laughed. "I wanted to see you. I've missed you."

I blushed.

As we walked, she told me everything about her trial starting from the moment she left me under the willow tree. Her trial had lasted only a few minutes, as she'd said before she left.

"Why didn't it last longer?" I asked.

"It didn't need to be that long. Zeus wasn't there, only the Moirai."

"Why?"

She shrugged.

Could it be because the war Apria had spoken of had begun? Could that mean the Titans really had found a way to escape Tartarus?

I felt Ashton's eyes on me.

"Are you worried about something?" she asked.

"Do I need to be?"

She shrugged again.

"Do you remember what you told me before you left? About the Lambdas' destinies not being able to be foreseen by the Moirai?" I asked.

She nodded.

"Is that why you've been given a second chance?"

She laughed and wrapped her arm around mine as we kept walking. "You don't think my destiny is pure?"

I grinned at her teasing. "I don't think they were able to see your destiny."

She smiled at that. "Maybe I have no destiny. Maybe there is no destiny to be seen? Or maybe I have many destinies."

She let go of my arm to hold my hand and started to skip, pulling me with her as I dragged my feet. She let go of my hand upon reaching the willow tree and sat me down in the dewy grass, then sat next to me. Even though the summer air at midnight was warm, she cuddled against me like it was midwinter.

"Did you miss me?" she asked.

I felt my brow furrowed deep within my forehead. The night she'd left, I'd thought there was no one I would miss more. Now that she was in front of me, I was truly missing another. Though I did miss Ashton's friendship, I missed something even more than her presence—her touch. When she awoke me with it, I felt the yearning then, and as she held me now, I was yearning for it even more. Her touch awakened a fire in my skin and between my thighs. Was it lust again?

I nodded. "I did."

She kissed me there and then. Unlike when kissing Troy, Taylor's face did not pop up in my mind, but lust still waded in my stomach, making it ache and flip. She laid me down in the grass and kissed me with a passion that told me how much she had missed me. I soon forgot about my stomachache.

She began to caress me where I felt my fire, gently yet ardently. She breathed softly into my ear. As the fire grew, her breaths grew faster as well, as if her breath fed my fire. She kissed my ear and took my earlobe into her mouth. My body shivered, and I lost my breath.

I need air. Her lips moved down to my neck. *I can't breathe.*

And then her mouth met mine and I sank into her embrace. Shuddering, I let out a moan and then gasped. She held me. All I wanted was for her to hold me. She began to kiss my cheeks, softly taking in my skin with her lips, and then gently kissed my mouth again. Her lips were wet and salty on mine. I looked up, and in the glistening of the moon, saw that her lips were wet with tears. Not her tears, but mine.

"Are you okay?" she asked.

I nodded and smiled, faking enough to convince her. But I was not okay. My tears had been falling without any warning lately, and I could barely keep track of the causes. I reached out to caress her, but she held my hand down.

"Just lay with me," she whispered.

Without any words, we lay in the grass under the willow tree holding each other. The Gods had blessed me again. Only a few days ago I was lying here with Ashton, thinking it might be our last sunset together. And now here we were watching the sunrise.

I would have been content to stay under the willow tree all day, but we both had to go to work. Ashton must have been thinking the same thing because she stood up suddenly, fixed her clothes, and turned to look at me with a smile.

"Let's go," she said reaching for my hand.

Instead of leading me back toward the school, she led me away. I felt like I was in a trance and didn't argue with her, didn't care if we missed work. I said nothing, just let her lead me.

I'd let her take me anywhere.

The thought startled me.

We reached a trailhead half a mile outside campus. Ashton went far into the trail, and I followed behind her, curious as to where she was taking me. She seemed to be searching for something. I didn't think to ask what; I was still in a daze, comparing her touch to Troy's. She turned off the trail, onto another that led even deeper into the forest.

Fallen trees and rotten trunks crowded around us, forcing us to either jump or go around them. After hopping off a big fallen tree, we reached a lazy stream about fifteen feet wide. Ashton knelt next to it. She cupped her hands and took a drink. I knelt and did the same, taking in the sweet taste of the stream water and the fresh scent of trees. When I looked up and saw Ashton beginning to undress, my mouth fell open.

"What are you doing?"

She gave me a big grin before pulling off her shirt and tossing it to me, then went into the stream and started washing herself. I eyed the Lambda brand on her shoulder blade. It was thick and embossed, very noticeable from afar. She acted as if it was something to show off, something to be proud of, while the Elders saw it as heinous, monstrous, and forbidden.

All for love. Controversies, banishment, torture. It was all because of love.

"Why do you always look at me with those eyes," she said.

"Which pair?" I teased.

She smiled softly, staring right at me with the most beautiful gaze. "The pair that makes me breathless."

My cheeks warmed. I had lost count of how many times she'd made me blush. As I felt the blood rush to my face and the stream's cool water flow past my ankles, I was suddenly overcome with the vision of Peitho and the Goddess bathing in the brook on the island of Petra. I remembered Peitho's sweet words.

As if a songbird in the forest had sung the answer to me, I finally recalled where I'd heard that name before. My brother John told me about her the day he took me to my father's shack. She was a relative of Aphrodite—the Goddess of Persuasion and Seduction.

Could Ashton be…?

But I thought twice before saying anything. I wanted to choose my words carefully. It was a shot in the dark.

"You remind me of someone when you speak like that," I told her.

She splashed some water on her face and then dipped her hair in the stream. "Oh?"

"Yes," I said, "an ancient Goddess."

She giggled. "And which one would that be?"

"Peitho," I said calmly. "You remind me of the Goddess Peitho."

She was combing her fingers in her hair when she suddenly stopped and looked at me.

"Peitho, huh?" Her eyes wandered, looking past me and around me into the trees, and then returned to stare deep into mine. "We should go."

∞

Ashton went to work, but I decided to go home, feeling ready to talk to Jaden, Nick, and Ricky about what Poseidon had shown me. We said our goodbyes and as she turned around, I felt her fear.

Of what?

I walked up the street, not knowing exactly where to start my story of what Poseidon had shown me. I still didn't know what it all meant.

I opened the door and stepped through the threshold, feeling heavy anxiety and fear. I didn't get too far into the house before Jaden came rushing toward me. She grabbed my shoulders and started shoving me back.

"You must go, Petra!" she shouted.

"What? Leave?"

"Yes," she cried. "We don't have time!"

"Why?"

"She's coming back!"

She?

Jaden spun me around before I could ask who she was talking about. She pushed me out the door, and then spun me around again. With one hand, she stuffed something in my mouth.

"Quick, eat this!"

I began to chew, and the gelatin-goo-like fruit hit my senses. Immediately, the ambrosia flowed through my veins, making my powers more acute.

"Quick. Go!" With that, she ran back into the house and slammed the door behind her.

What the hell?

My mouth had been hanging open the whole time. I was completely and utterly confused. But as soon as I turned back around to face the street, I knew who she was talking about. Allison was standing in the middle of the road. We locked eyes. I had never seen eyes so dark. Tear tracks lined her cheeks. She began to walk toward me, and I could not help but move toward her, as if we were opposing magnets.

As each step brought me closer to her, the nectar's power grew even stronger in me. My senses were electric, my atoms vibrating. I didn't tear my gaze from Allison's, but I could tell my body was glowing just as strongly as hers. It was as if the sun's light had burst inside me. I felt so strong and powerful, and I felt her power as well. She gritted her teeth, her hands clenched, and the power of her anger washed over me, pounding loudly beneath the pavement.

Why is she angry?

It all happened quickly yet felt as if it was in slow motion. When we were ten feet apart, a purple bubble appeared around her. Its energy painfully pierced my senses, confusing me greatly. I recoiled from its power, but the core of my body began to feel tantalizingly warm until an answering circle of green began growing around me, holding the same powerful energy.

We got closer and closer, closing the gap faster and faster. We were still several feet apart when our bubbles of energy touched, and then erupted. A light as bright as lightning exploded out from us, and our bodies were flung backwards. A loud explosion echoed. I found myself stuck into the metal of our garage door. I looked down the street and saw that Allison had been flung into a car. The street where we had stood just a second ago was destroyed, along with everything in a ten-yard radius, as if a meteor had hit the residential street.

Allison was up and in front of me before I even got myself out of the garage door. She grabbed my neck and pulled me out, holding me above her head so my toes dangled, barely touching the driveway. Through her hand around my throat, I felt her sorrow and pain. I reached for her hands and tried to move my head to look at her. I was able to stare deep into her eyes.

"Why?" I asked

With little movement of her body, and as if I were nothing but a paper plane, she threw me back into the garage door. This time, I went through it and into the back wall of our garage, leaving an indentation of my body in the wall.

What would have knocked a mortal out cold, I barely felt because of the ambrosia. She picked me up and threw me again. That one stung a bit as my back caught on the hook that hung Jaden's bike. Her throwing me around did cause some pain to my body, but not as much as it did to my mind. I strained my gifts to search her reasons for doing this.

I shook off the cement wall pieces and began to stand up, but Allison was too quick; she was in front of me again, reaching for my throat once more. She helped me up, again holding me off the ground. This time I was ready for her. With speed like lightning, I swung both hands in a circular motion to the insides of her arms and smacked her wrists as if I were chopping them. Her hands immediately released from my neck, and she grunted with pain. I continued the circular motion of my hands out, and then in toward me and then out, hitting both palms against her chest. The movement was quick and powerful.

I pushed her with a force that nearly knocked the soul out of her. Her body flew backwards and shot out of the garage. I followed her out and tackled her before she was able to completely stand on both feet. Our bodies tumbled down the driveway and into the middle of the cratered street. She twisted my arm and cupped my throat. I felt her heartbeat pulsing through her fingertips. She lifted me up and slammed the back of my head on the street. A great pain exploded from my skin. I wondered if I was bleeding.

My hands came up to my throat to grab her hand and twist it. I had her locked in my grip, and I spun her around, holding her arm out away from her body. I shoved her face into the pavement. I had never fought someone before, but I did love watching the wrestling events at our winter and summer solstice parties. I imagined I'd learned these moves from that—that, and the ambrosia. I felt it telling me what to do and giving me the strength to do it.

I had her pinned, her face squished against the street. I knelt to look into her eyes, darkened by anger and pain.

Why?

My grip loosened just for a second, and she nearly shoved me off. She was so strong, but thankfully, I was in the better position and forced her down harder with my knee against her back. I needed more time to feel her and figure out where her anger was coming from.

"Why are you doing this, Allison?" I muttered against her back.

Perhaps I lost my concentration, or she was just too strong, but her wrists slipped from my hands and she slammed both palms into my chest, making me shoot into the sky. My body flailed as I flew into the air, as if I was swimming in the sky. I didn't get too high before she shot up from the ground and grabbed me while still in the air. Our bodies slammed onto the roof of our house. She was on top and had me pinned down against the roof's tiling with my head dangling over the ledge.

Allison bent down very close to my face, and my eyes met hers. The caramel brown had turned almost amber from her anger. I tried again, searching for the cause of her pain. Then tears started to form under her eyelids, and I watched as the puddle grew enough that I could see my own reflection in it. I could even make out what expression my face was making. A single tear fell onto my cheek, and in that tear, I finally sensed where her anger came from. She knew. She'd found out about Ashton and me, and she felt betrayed—by me and by love.

She gripped my shirt and held my eyes. I wanted her to do it. I deserved it. She knew the fall wouldn't kill me, but she wished it would.

"O' by the Gods, Allison," a voice said from below the roof. "Let her speak."

We tore our eyes from one another to look at Jaden, who stood with her hands on her hips, scowling.

About time she came. Some guardian.

"No words can undo this," Allison whispered. "No words."

She rose off me, brushed herself and her tears off, and then jumped from the roof, landing softly on her toes. She stopped to look at Jaden, and I could feel her louder than before. I twisted around to my stomach and watched Allison's back as she ran down the street. Tears started to stream down my face, not for myself or for what just happened. They were not my tears I was crying, but Allison's. Her hurt was uncontrollable. She wanted to destroy me, and she would have succeeded.

Jaden was looking at me. Her hands were still on her hips, but her face had changed to a solemn expression, as if I were a child caught doing something I shouldn't. I stood and wobbled a bit, my body already feeling sore. I jumped down from the roof and landed on the cracked pavement, then stumbled over to Jaden.

"So that's what you were trying to warn me about?" I asked, still rubbing my neck.

She nodded, and then slowly started to shake her head. "What was that about?"

"I deserved it."

Jaden kept shaking her head. Then she reached in her back pocket and took out an orange gel tablet, which she held out on her palm. "This is ambrosia. I was able to get some made into tablets for easier consumption."

I gave her a sideways glance before taking it from her hand. "Is that what held you up from saving me?"

A ghost of a smile appeared on her face.

"Did you see what happened?" I asked as I chucked the pill in my mouth and swallowed.

As soon as I swallowed, the bright glow of my body was revived, and the soreness went away. My body felt rejuvenated instantly.

"Only the last bit of you two on the roof." She looked around. "Did an asteroid crash?"

"This damage," I told her while looking around, "was all from something I've never seen or felt before."

"What do you mean?"

"Her anger—it was so powerful. I've never felt anger that strong before. Her anger somehow took form as a thin purplish bubble, a force of some sort that surrounded her."

Jaden went still. I had all her attention.

I continued, "And then the most unexplainable thing happened—my body reacted to it. To the purple thing, and I started growing one too, but it was green. Our energy bubbles touched and exploded into the brightest light, and then we shot apart from each other."

She gasped. "I've never heard of that happening."

"I've never seen such things either," I replied.

"What does it mean?"

"I was hoping you'd know, my guardian," I quipped.

She shook her head. "I don't." Her eyes looked past me, as if she were really concentrating on whatever was behind me. Then her eyes grabbed mine. "What caused her to be so angry?"

I cringed, but said nothing.

"Does it have to do with a midnight visit from Ashton?" she asked curtly, giving me a start.

How does she know? "Did you tell Allison?"

"No!" she shouted, and then paused. "I do deserve an explanation though, do I not?"

I gave her another wary sideways glance. She gave me a concerned look back that twisted my stomach, and I nodded slowly.

"Ashton returned last night from her judgment trial."

I heard her soft gasp but didn't want to look at her face.

"She's a Lambda?"

I nodded. "So is Allison."

She gasped again, cupping her hand over her mouth.

"Allison and Ashton were lovers," I said.

"Are you now Ashton's lover?"

I finally looked up at her. "No!" I shouted angrily. "She's my friend. Nothing more."

Then I paused in my own thoughts. *Why am I so defensive?*

My anger started to cease and then, slowly, I answered, "I care for her." I paused again. "Very much. As she does for me." I took in a deep breath. "I don't love her like that."

There was no better or worse way to explain how I felt about Ashton. No diagram, no formula, and no equation to help elaborate the feelings we had for one another. It was unspoken. Just felt.

Jaden gazed at me as if I was the stars, as if I was someone other than myself. I thought she hadn't heard me. And I was more talking to myself anyway. I hadn't expected an answer from her. But after a long pause, she finally nodded.

"Someone must have told Allison," I mumbled. I knew it; I felt it in my gut.

There was a long silence, each of us working on our own thoughts.

"I wish you hadn't come home early from work," she finally said. "Why did you?"

"I had to talk to you and Nick about some things."

"Yeah," she said. "Nick and I have some things to discuss with you, too."

She looked past me again and waved her hand in a gesture for someone to come. Before I could ask what she was doing, I felt Nick behind me, and he was not happy with me at all.

"In the mood for a little trip?" he asked.

Without waiting for my response, he grabbed me by the collar, scooped Jaden into his arms, and shot up into the sky.

∞

We landed on soft sand. Before I even looked up, I knew where we were, though I had only been here in dreams and visions. The sand felt just as it did in my visions, the salt from the sea tingling in my nose, and the same trees waved in the breeze. I breathed it all in. Just as fresh, just as beautiful and my body welcomed it. Their eyes were on me, watching me cautiously while letting me take in the island.

"Do you know where you are?" Jaden asked.

I nodded. "It's familiar," I said with a smile.

"This is really it then?" Nick asked. "The island from your dreams?"

I nodded again, still with the biggest grin on my face. "It is."

"You know what this place is called?" Jaden asked.

I finally looked away from the paradise and looked deep into their eyes one at a time. "It's the island called Petra."

"Is that its name?" Nick asked.

I nodded. "How did you know about this island?"

"After Poseidon sent you here, he gave Nick the coordinates to find you. He found you on the shore, passed out, and brought you back home."

"You brought me home?" I asked.

He nodded. "I tried going back there, just to check it out. I checked the coordinates several times, but it wasn't there anymore. So—"

"That's because it always moves," I interrupted, then turned to look back out at the trees.

"Yes," Jaden muttered. "How did you know that?"

I turned to her and gave her a smile. "Because Peitho said so. How did you find it again?"

"Jaden asked Poseidon for the updated coordinates."

"I thought it wasn't real," I said. "I thought I was in some kind of hologram scene that Poseidon wanted me to see. But if you found me here, then I'm not exactly sure what was real and what wasn't."

"What?" they asked simultaneously.

"One moment I was standing in front of Poseidon, and the next I was standing on this island. At first, I thought I was just dreaming about the hooded woman again, but then I heard voices in the trees and followed them to a brook."

I wonder…

I stopped talking and started walking to where I had followed the voices. Jaden and Nick followed. I saw the brook from a distance and immediately started running toward it. I reached the water and spotted the big boulder I'd hidden behind.

"I came here," I ran toward the boulder, "and hid."

"Hid from what?" Jaden asked.

"From the two Goddesses bathing in this brook. One was dark haired and the other had golden hair." I pointed a little bit upstream to where I could still envision them. "At first I couldn't understand what they were saying. They spoke the old language. But then a soft light came from the Heavens and I was granted the ability to understand them."

I smiled, remembering it so clearly. I looked at Nick and Jaden and saw them smiling too.

"The golden-haired Goddess was saying she was scared of someone."

"Of who?" Nick asked.

"The dark-haired Goddess's sister, I think. But she kept assuring the other one not to be afraid. She said her sister could never find out about them because the island is endlessly buoyant." I smiled, remembering Peitho's last words, and decided to leave that part out. "Then the golden-haired one said they have this island to thank. She called it Petra. I thought they must have spotted me and therefore were calling for me, but then I realized they couldn't see me. I was nothing but a ghost walking among them."

"Who were they?" Nick pressed.

"The dark-haired Goddess was called Peitho, but I don't know who the other one was."

Nick gasped, and Jaden began to pace back and forth.

"What was Poseidon's reason for showing you this?" she muttered.

She was talking to herself, but that didn't keep me from responding. "I asked myself the same thing."

Jaden kept pacing as Nick held his chin inquisitively.

"There's more," I said softly.

Jaden stopped pacing, and they both looked at me.

"Apria, or Aphrodite, was there too, hidden in the trees over there." I pointed farther upstream into the overgrown myrtle where I'd seen her. "And she looked awfully angry."

"Aphrodite!" Jaden said loudly. "That's who Peitho was talking about!"

I nodded, affirming Jaden's hypothesis. *Peitho was—*

"Aphrodite's sister is Peitho," Jaden said aloud.

"Yes." I nodded again. "The other Goddess was scared of Peitho's sister… Aphrodite."

"Someone definitely to be scared of in ancient times—still to be scared of," Nick mumbled.

I wanted to ask him what he meant, but Jaden's question distracted me. "But what was she doing on the island?"

"More importantly, why was she so pissed off when she saw Peitho and the other Goddess together?" I asked. "And why was the Goddess scared of Aphrodite to begin with?"

We fell silent. Sounds of the water flowing down the brook, songbirds singing in the trees, and small creatures and insects crawling aimlessly on the island floor were all I heard.

"Okay, let's go," Jaden said suddenly.

"Where?" Nick asked.

I was wondering the same thing.

"Back to the Library of Alexandria," Jaden said with a smile, "to learn more about this Peitho."

Chapter 13

The Three Loves

We entered the Library of Alexandria the same way we had before. Even the second time, I was just as astounded by its greatness, and I noticed more things than I had the first time. The great garden behind me had trees of varying sizes and shapes. Several tree trunks resembled articulated braids, wrapping up and around to the top where they burst out, sprouting leaves of vivid green and gold. Other trees grew outward, like thick vines spiraling down the path. Plants lined both sides of the pathway, some in luscious colors I'd never known plants could be. There were flowers in all the colors of the rainbow; some looked deadly, with teeth and needles, while others were as soft as cotton.

I studied the archaic statues at the ends of the rows of bookshelves. The massive statues of great warriors represented every era. They wore armor from all different cultures around the world, and even some I had never seen on this planet. The statues seemed fresh and alive, just as they must have thousands or even hundreds of thousands of years ago. Each was from a different world, each keeping guard over the histories of their own kind.

We walked down the main aisle, passing where we'd searched for Aphrodite's account. Halfway down, the aisle seemed to grow longer. The end disappeared into the darkness, miles away. A couple of yards from me, a podium held an extremely large and thick book. Jaden and Nick stopped walking once they found the row they were looking for, but I continued toward the podium that held the extraordinary book.

I blew the dust from the cover and read the title. "*The Akashic Record of Accounts*... What's this?"

Nick and Jaden didn't answer right away, and I felt their internal conflict.

"It's a book of accounts," Nick said.

Obviously, I thought, but, "Oh," was all I said.

I brushed my fingers over the gold-plated cover. The writing was a beautiful cursive embossed in white gold. I opened it slowly. The font was the tiniest gold cursive script, barely legible, but filling the entire page from top to bottom with no margin on either side.

I moved my face closer to the page, almost touching it with my nose. I could finally make out a name, and as Nick said, after it was an account of everything they had done in their entire life—down to the smallest detail. There was another name and their account, and then another name, and so on. I went to turn the page and stopped to feel the texture on my fingers. The pages were thin, very thin, as if I was holding nothing. A material I could not understand.

"Whose accounts are these?" I asked, still flicking through the weightless pages.

"Everyone's," Jaden said.

"Everyone's?"

"Every mortal human in this physical world," Nick added.

I closed it quickly, suddenly feeling I had done something wrong, like I was peeking in on someone's private life—or everyone's private life.

"Everyone's?" I repeated softly. My hand reached for the book again.

Will I find Taylor's account in this book? My fingers held the cover as my mind contemplated the thought. *Should I look?*

Temptation wrapped its fingers around me, urging me to search for her name. I would discover everything about her, every detail. All the answers I had ever wanted were just under my fingertips.

Suddenly, someone grabbed my hand.

"We found Peitho's account," Nick said, holding my hand, which was still on the cover. I could feel the urgency in his touch. He lured me away from the great book and my curiosity suddenly disappeared.

Jaden slammed Peitho's account on the table. "Petra, I want to tell you something before we read this."

I nodded for her to continue.

She closed her eyes and let out a deep sigh, then opened her eyes and looked deeply into mine. "Whatever we find out, just know my duty to you is determined by Poseidon. If he has willed you to see this, then it is in your destiny to discover it. I will always stand by you and go wherever your destiny leads you."

Her words filled my chest with joy, and sparked warmth deep within my soul. Her words gave me strength. I think we all felt it then. This was something grave. How we'd gotten here was beyond me. It seemed that the more we asked questions and tried to find answers, the more deeply we were being led into something serious. This was something we were not prepared for. I was not prepared for. Yet, with them next to me, it was easier to be on this journey of discovering who I was. Who I am. I didn't feel alone. I closed my eyes. Thank the Gods for Nick and Jaden.

I opened my eyes and met Jaden's. "Thank you."

She nodded with a smile, went to open the book but then hesitated. "Do you want to read it?"

My breath stopped, as if it too was waiting for my answer.

"Yes," I said, resoundingly.

She nodded and pushed the book across the table to me.

"Peitho: The Goddess of Persuasion and Seduction," I read aloud.

As I read her name, something came over me. I brushed my fingers over the lettering as if touching her. Touching the life she'd lived, only to become words in a dusty book. I felt an intense connection then and brushed my teardrop from the cover before opening it.

There were ripped edges in the back of the book. Immediately I flipped to the end. All the back pages were gone—completely torn from the binding.

"It's gone," I said, holding the book wide open.

"What the hell?" Nick and Jaden said almost simultaneously.

"What does that mean?" I asked worriedly.

"I don't understand," Jaden said, perplexed.

"It means someone doesn't want that to be read," Nick answered.

"Who's trying to hide Peitho's account?" Jaden asked softly.

I shook my head. "At least there are still some pages." I flipped back to the beginning and starting reading.

"Born from Mother Earth, Gaia, and Father Sky, Uranus, they came from the sea. One soul split into three, formed Eros, Peitho, and Aphrodite. Their gifts came from love and all its designs. They were the most beautiful and significant of their time... they were the Three Loves, one of each kind."

I skimmed a few lines down and read some more.

"Great controversy arose in the Heavens. The new generation of Gods split to eleven and named themselves the Olympians. They did not conform to the Titans' rule. Zeus, leader of the Olympians, soon challenged his father, Cronus, to a duel. Thus began the revolution.

"Massacre occurred within Cronus's kingdom, threatening the existence of the Primordial Gods and Titans, and forced the three siblings to flee. Eros escaped into the heart of the mountain. Peitho and Aphrodite fled to the sea.

"Aphrodite was quickly captured, but Peitho escaped with the aid of the Titan Oceanus. Centuries after the war, Aphrodite found Peitho..."

I flipped the page. "That's it. The rest is gone."

"Well that didn't really give us any help," Jaden said.

"I guess what's torn out would have," Nick added.

"Well, *we* know what ended up happening to Aphrodite. It said there were eleven Olympians before the war. We know Aphrodite was the twelfth one. And we know that she's still alive and among the young."

Jaden and I nodded in agreement with Nick.

"And it tells us why she was mad!" I said excitedly.

They looked at me with tilted heads.

"Well, sort of." I paused. "I wonder if in the dream I was witnessing Aphrodite finding Peitho." I stopped to think about it. "Then I can see why Aphrodite would be angry. All this time, Aphrodite was probably looking for Peitho, worried sick, thinking she was in trouble or in danger, but Peitho was happy and content with someone else when she saw her."

"But that doesn't make sense," Nick muttered. "Why would the other Goddess be scared of Aphrodite then?"

"That's right," Jaden interjected. "The other Goddess knew Aphrodite was her sister and must have known she was looking for Peitho."

We looked at each other, hoping to find the answers in one another's eyes.

Nick shook his head, "I wish the book could tell us more!"

"I wish the book could tell us who the other Goddess was with Peitho," Jaden said. "What did the other Goddess look like?"

I shook my head. "I couldn't get a good look at her face. Her back was facing me most of the time."

"What was she wearing?" Nick asked.

"Nothing," I said, my tone matter of fact.

They both tensed up and blushed. "But she had long golden hair with a flower wreath in it." I sighed. "Peitho sure did look a lot like Ashton Janus," I muttered. "Maybe Ashton is the one who ripped out these pages."

Jaden's mouth dropped open. "You think Ashton could be of Peitho's bloodline?"

I shrugged. "No, I think maybe it's her reincarnated. She acts just like her."

Nick gave an exasperated snort.

"What's funny?" Jaden snapped.

"I think we're in way over our heads on this." He snickered. "Peitho is an ancient one. The book says she's a Primordial Goddess, which means she was part of the first. I doubt that even reincarnated she would want to be among the young, let alone on Earth."

"Well why not?" Jaden said. "Aphrodite is still among the young."

"That's just Aphrodite, though," Nick said. "And she's only been seen by you and Petra, not the mortals. Ashton goes to a mortal school."

Jaden sighed and nodded in agreement.

"Why, is it not common for an ancient God or Goddess to live among mortal humans?" As I spoke, I remembered Ashton's words when I asked her if Allison Prome was a Titanide.

"There are many Titanides living among you, my dear."

Shivers went down my spine.

Nick and Jaden shook their heads, almost instantly.

"Absolutely not," Nick said. "They're too strong to go unnoticed by humans. Gaianus taught the younger generation how to live among humans peacefully. That was its whole purpose. But most of the original Primordial Gods and Titans have either been sent to Tartarus, ascended back home to the stars, or are in the Elder council."

"What about Theia?" I asked softly.

"Theia is one of the Elders in the council," Nick replied.

"She's also my boss," I said. "At Regis." I had their attention now. "How is she on Earth and playing a mortal role?"

Nick was finally speechless. They both slowly shook their heads, dumbfounded. With two Titanides and possibly a reincarnated Primordial Goddess walking among us, I could not stop myself from thinking of what Apria and Dion had told me about the Elder Olympians being on the brink of war.

Have the Titans really found a way to escape Tartarus and challenge the Olympians with an army?

Once again, I remembered Ashton's words, which fit perfectly alongside my train of thought.

Lambdas' destinies are always unclear and changing.

Could Lambdas be the Titans' new destined avengers? This couldn't all be a coincidence, could it? Were we on the brink of another revolution?

Chapter 14

A Choice of Two Evils

The house was as tense as the continuous knot in my stomach. There was a time when I didn't want to be on Earth. Now Allison made me wish I had never even existed. The remorse I felt, on top of sensing her pain every time I entered the house, drew me into a kind of insanity where I wished for oblivion. I could no longer look into her eyes nor be in the same room as her. A friendship as good as ours once was had ceased to exist.

It was a new sort of pain I had not been acquainted with before, and I found I could not bear it on a daily basis. We never again spoke of what had happened in front of our house that day. I still didn't know what the energy bubble was or how it had come to be.

I started praying to Chronos as I began to write: *'I'm sorry Allison. I am so sorry.'*

My mind slipped into a negative space as I remembered how I'd even gotten to where I was. If only I had not allowed this to happen. If only I was smarter than Ashton and didn't fall for her enchantments. If only I'd never started feeling my emotions. If only I'd never kissed Taylor. If only that kiss hadn't birthed these emotions. If only I hadn't come to this mortal school.

Would Chronos find me needy? Was I asking too much?

'If only time could rewind my regret away,' I wrote.

I opened and closed the note several times, and before I put the pen down, I took one last look at it. A breath escaped my chest, and without further thought, I tucked the note under my pillow. Allison's eyes would never see it.

∞

That night, someone called my name through the darkness. My eyelids barely started opening when I heard her call again.

"Petra," Jaden whispered. "Petra, wake up."

I rubbed the sleep out of my eyes and sat up in bed.

"Someone's outside," she said. "Someone for you."

I looked out our bedroom window and saw a silhouetted body standing under the moonlight.

"Petra." I looked back to Jaden. "Please be careful."

I nodded and quietly stepped out of our bedroom. The air had a haunting chill to it. I breathed it in, and it smelled like rain, though I saw no clouds, only some of the constellations and the full moon. It reminded me of the last time I'd seen her. It felt like longer than one moon cycle. I considered the possibility that either she'd been avoiding someone, me specifically, or that Allison had forbidden her to see me.

I stopped a couple of feet in front of her, thinking that if I avoided catching a glimpse of her eyes, I would be safe.

"Where have you been?" I asked.

She moved closer to me, but I stepped back.

"You left me, Ashton." I paused. "You left me alone... to deal with this."

"I know," she said breathlessly.

"What happened to you?" My voice cracked.

"She came to me after she fought with you..." She tried stepping closer and then stopped. "She made me choose, Petra."

"Choose?" I was still whispering.

"A choice of two evils," she said, laughing pathetically. "Either leave Earth and go back home, or stay and be bound to her. So I chose the lesser one."

"*Doulus*," I muttered in our language. A slave.

She shrugged. "Both choices leave me doomed." She let out a small, uneven breath. "Both choices ultimately won't give me you," she said softly, as if it she had just now come to that realization.

Those words made me want to cry, but I fought hard not to let tears fall in front of her.

"But I chose to be bound to her, because at least I'd still get to see you."

I stepped away from her and felt the house against my back. My legs gave in and I sank down, burying my head in my knees.

"But you're a prisoner," I whispered. I lifted my eyes to hers. "But of your body or your heart?"

She said nothing. My tears began to revolt, and I fought even harder for none to fall.

"Oh, Petra," she whispered. She sat down against the wall next to me. "Let us be done with this lustful dance."

"Wha-" I choked out. My voice filled with anger. "We are so sure to call it that?" My face fell into my hands.

"Well, it isn't love." She laughed.

My chest gave way, pressing into my lungs until I choked. Ashton reached out and touched the back of her hand to my cheek.

"I've seen how love looks from these eyes," she said, lifting my face to hers.

"Love?" I asked. "Who?"

She laughed softly, beautifully. "I believe Miss Taylor Letto has that honor."

I jerked my head away from her hand. The name fell from her tongue lightly, but carried a weight that settled heavily on my chest. Once again, it began to open as a flower does for the sun's rays.

"Since when?" I asked, through gritted teeth.

"I don't know when it started happening for you," she said. "I only know when I began to notice it."

She moved away from the wall to position herself in front of me. "It was that night at the bar. The look on your face when you saw her could have made even the Goddess of Love embrace you." She smiled to herself. "I could never forget it. From that day on, every time you looked at me, I searched your eyes for that look." A ghost of a teasing smile came upon her lips. "But I never did find it."

I felt her sadden. She brought her knees close to her chest and wrapped her arms around them, as if to protect her heart.

I didn't say anything. I didn't know how to respond to that. I hadn't known any truth in it, though I hadn't known any lie either. And for that moment, my ambivalence frightened me.

Do I love Taylor Letto?

I froze in that thought.

Ashton must have seen me not take a breath; she grabbed both my hands, brought them to her lips, and kissed the tops of them gently.

"Petra." She was staring at me. At the same time, my will finally gave in and let go, letting all my rebellious tears fall. I just felt so much: sad, confused, hurt, betrayed. Was this the power of Peitho? Hadn't she seduced me enough?

"Look at me," Ashton said.

121

My tears would not let me. I was so embarrassed of them. I did all I could to hide them.

"Please?" she pleaded—persuaded—sweetly.

With that plea, there was nothing more I could do, and so I looked up.

"Everything will be okay," she said with a grin. "I promise."

∞

After that night, I spent most nights watching the sky change; it was the only thing that gave me peace.

Allison's feelings toward me were as predictable as the passing of the sun, but some days were worse than others. The good days were when I was avoiding her or she was avoiding me. Knowing that she slept a door down from me kept me awake at night. She wouldn't hurt me, but knowing I gave her good enough reason to was what held my eyelids open.

We had an unexpected day off at work, and I sensed it was going to be a bad day. I kept myself busy with unnecessary errands throughout the morning until I ran out of things to do at lunch. I was coming back from the laundromat carrying a couple bags of clothes when I saw her. I turned the corner out of the mat and there she was. How could a tiny Goddess be so intimidating? Even from a few yards away I could sense her strength. She was so strong and held so much power. And she gazed upon me with such disgust that I wanted to cry right where I stood. I had to look away from her immediately, but then I noticed who was standing with her.

Troy looked as if someone had just knocked the wind out of him. My body let out a cry. Immediately, I became weak at the thought of what she could be telling him. Red veins surrounded his blue eyes. My stomach was choking on my lungs.

She told him.

I wanted to run to him and beg for his forgiveness. My gut had no doubt about what my eyes were witnessing. Then he met my eyes. If I had eaten lunch, my stomach would have thrown it to the pavement. I looked into Troy's eyes and saw in them the same disgust I saw in Allison's.

What am I to do with myself? How am I to fix this now?

It was then that a cloud, or more like a green hazy fog, began to climb into my vision. I stared deeper into Troy's eyes as the fog began to turn everything

122

green. I begged him to hear me, and to my surprise, he blinked a couple of times and lifted his head up to me.

Had he heard me? The thought shocked even me.

I was taught that only the ancient Gods had telepathy. The younger Gods were never given such gifts. Or was that another lie Gaianus had told us? I quickly discarded that thought, and as the green kept creeping into my vision, making it hard to see Troy's face, I prayed for him to hear me.

Please, I thought again, a*llow me to explain. Tonight at the pool?*

I stared at him, praying to the Gods that he had heard me. He gave a start and then stared at me for a couple of seconds before giving me a discreet nod.

∞

I paced back and forth in front of my lifeguard post, nerves in a frenzy, hands clenched, gnawing on my bottom lip. I couldn't decide if I was angrier with Allison for telling Troy or at the fact that I had developed nerves. I had never been anxious before, and my bottom lip suffered for it. What was taking him so long?

Suddenly the door swung open. I sensed his anguish immediately and bit down harder on my lip, flooding my tongue with the taste of blood before my lip repaired itself.

There was no withholding the truth this time. Whether I was ready for it or not, I needed honesty to prevail. He deserved the truth.

"I'm glad you came—"

"I'm not," he snapped.

I looked at him. "Well, I'm glad you did."

He walked to the edge of the pool, kicked off his sandals, and sat down. He let his feet dangle into the water.

"What has Allison told you?" I asked.

He took off his shirt, folded it up, and set it beside him before answering. "She told me you're screwing her ex-girlfriend," he said sharply, and then plopped into the pool with a splash.

My body recoiled at his words. His anger was a stab to my chest. I gulped.

"Yes." It was hard to admit. "I was."

Instantly, I sensed his hope. He spun around to face me. "Not anymore?"

I was confused. Why was hope greeting my senses instead of disgust, instead of shame?

I shook my head. "No." I stared at the ground. "Not anymore."

His warmth made me want to cry.

Why, by the Gods, is he so happy about this?

He jumped out of the pool and came to me. He held me at arm's length and bent his head down to meet my eyes, which were staring at his glistening, perfect chest.

"Then I want you, Petra," he said.

"What?" His response shocked me greatly.

The ego of an Athlete God overwhelmed my senses. When I'd seen him standing with Allison, his ego had taken a hit, but it wasn't beaten. I felt sick to my stomach. There was nothing more unsatisfying to sense. I was sickened by my own actions—more than him, even more than Allison. He should not forgive me for this. What I had done was a sin against the Gods, against Zeus and his law. How could Troy not see that?

"I don't care about Ashton. If you're saying you and she are over, then tell me now, Petra," he paused, "will you be with me?"

I was shocked even more. My mind couldn't catch up to what my ears were hearing. Certainly, he was joking.

"I-I laid with a woman, Troy…"

"Yes, I know."

"Does that not disgust you?"

"Are you lying with her now?" He stepped closer and grabbed me gently by my shoulders.

"No!" I said curtly.

"Do you still want to lie with her?"

I paused to think about the question. I was certain I would miss her touch, but…

"No."

The truth stung. Although it hurt me, it was true. I did not want to lie with her anymore.

His hope grew stronger with my answer. I did not understand where this was coming from.

"Then will you be with me?" he asked again.

"I-" I paused. "I don't know."

With that answer, my body slumped forward and gave way to uncertainty. Simultaneously, I sensed his confidence repairing fully. I had rejected him on multiple occasions, slept with a woman, and yet he did not care and still wanted to be with me. It was beyond fascinating to me.

"Do you love her?" he asked softly. "Are you branded?"

I stepped away from his grip and away from his warmth. I felt he knew the answer, and all the same, was excited as he waited for my affirmation. I didn't deserve it. I didn't deserve him.

The night Ashton had suggested we stop our lustful dance, I was shocked that she'd called it that. Although what I felt for Ashton was powerful and we had a strong connection, I had known deep down something was amiss. I had no clue what love felt like. All these emotions were so new to me. So if Ashton said that what we had was lust and not love, then I believed her.

"No," I told him finally, then let my face fall into my hands. Without even looking at him, I could sense his smile.

He stepped to me, took my hands from my face, and held them in his. "Petra," he said, softly, "the demons haven't left their mark on your body. Please don't allow them to leave one on your soul." He stepped even closer to me, gently put my hands on his cheeks, and looked into my eyes. "Let me cast them out."

Through my fingertips, I felt his sincerity, his tenderness, and his warmth. I didn't deserve it. I didn't deserve any of it.

He stopped my mind with his lips and began to kiss me with a passion that made me forget about Ashton, forget about Taylor, and forget about the hooded woman… for in that moment, I had him.

Chapter 15

Only a Dream

I could not get the taste of salt off my lips. I licked them continuously until they were too sensitive to touch. I was dehydrated and hungry. I had not eaten much since the day she left me. There was nothing my body needed more than her.

I waited in the same spot where we always met, under the crooked palm tree in the tall grassy knoll that overlooked the dock where she would tie up her sailboat. She came every new moon and two had passed since I had last seen her.

Has she gotten lost? I thought. When I was young, she told me the island floated everywhere, to the ends of the Earth and back. *Did the island move to a place she could not find?*

My mind was tired. The air had gotten too hot and it started playing tricks on me. I would imagine her boat tied to the dock, imagine I saw her standing in front of me, her tunic off and ready for us to celebrate her homecoming. My lips stung painfully as I tried smiling at the thought.

Sleep began to descend upon my body, but then quickly fear awoke me. *Has she been caught?* My body was too tired. Even though I feared for her life, my eyelids pulled down as the reminiscing began.

∞

I remembered the day she'd first told me she was in exile. I had known her for a year then. In that year, I still had not seen her face. So I asked her why she wore a hood, every day, all day, even when she slept. I asked her to take it off and she said no. When I persisted and pleaded with her, she became angry. With so much pain in her voice, she yelled it out then—that she was in hiding. I asked why, but she was evasive with her answers. I was eleven then.

I asked again when I was sixteen. It was on Winter Solstice. She'd given me scrolls and a charcoal stick as a gift, as usual, but all I wanted was for her to unveil herself. She became angry with me again. We started yelling. She made me so mad I threw my scrolls into the fire. She managed to rescue only one before they burned. That was the first night I saw her glowing, ocean-colored eyes misty with tears.

That was the night I fell in love with her.

I wrote my first poem on the charred scroll and gave it to her as a Winter Solstice gift. After she read it, I thought I saw her stone barrier began to crack. She made her way across the campfire, kissed my brow, and told me that one day she would be able to roam free without her hood. I asked when, but all she would say was, "Soon."

∞

My eyes opened and began stinging from the burning sun. I remembered those days as if they were yesterday. It had been ten years since I'd met her and four years since the night I'd realized I loved her. I wanted to smile at the thought, but my lips were so chapped and bloodied that they'd stuck together. I managed to look toward the dock, but was disheartened when I still didn't see her boat.

Suddenly, an overpowering despair came over me. She must have been caught. I knew it instantly in that moment. My heart fell to my feet and I grasped my chest. It felt like there was a dagger in it. I cried out with the most torturous scream that all the Gods could hear, for my soul felt destroyed and my heart severed from my body.

I wept in the sandy, tall grass for my beloved. No amount of tears could heal the sorrow. *Will I ever get her back?* The whole world I loved because she was in it was now shattered, dropping all its pieces around my falling tears.

Suddenly, a bright light broke through my eyelids. I opened my eyes and saw through my tears the Goddess of Love.

"Aphrodite!" I called. "O' my Goddess dove!"

"My child, why are you crying?" She came to me, scooped my weak body into her arms, and gently began rocking me.

"My beloved," I cried. "She has been taken from me!"

All of a sudden, Aphrodite stopped her rocking. "O' my child, she has not been taken."

My cries came to a halt, allowing me to dream, allowing me to hope her words were good and true, and that I had worried for nothing.

"She is pregnant with Zeus' child."

127

Suddenly a black void descended and swallowed up her words, along with my mind and my whole being. My breath was no more.

I saw my heart split in two and Aphrodite holding each piece in her palms. It seemed as though she was smiling, but she was not. There was only darkness. The darkness created by Zeus.

Growing up, I had heard his name a lot from my beloved. She had educated me very well about all the Gods and Goddesses. She'd never had anything good to say about him, and I never knew why. I always thought that if he was the ruler then he had to be good. She hated that I thought that.

Why would she love the God she'd claimed to hate? Was it because he'd broken her heart? Or because she was hiding her heart from love?

Suddenly it made sense. She wasn't hiding herself. She was hiding her heart. But now that she had finished educating me and looking after me, now that I was a young adult, she'd gone back to her true beloved. She had never truly loved me.

It was a tragedy. All those years wasted. She had played me for the ultimate ignorant fool in the game of love.

"Aphrodite, why," I cried. My life was worthless if she was not true. Love had no value anymore, and therefore neither did life.

I reached for the dagger on my belt and gripped it tightly. "Aphrodite, end it," I begged. "Please, Aphrodite, end it all."

∞

I woke up with a jerk. Instantly, I felt hot, shallow breaths on my neck and a heavy arm around my waist. I managed to turn around and saw that I was in Troy's arms. My memory began to come back to me. We had left the pool house and walked to his dorm room holding hands. There, I remembered falling asleep in his arms on the couch. He must have brought me to his bed.

Slowly I lifted his heavy arm off me and slid out. I saw I was still fully clothed and let out the biggest sigh. I spied my shoes near the couch, quickly put them on, and went out into the sunrise.

While walking home, I kept thinking about what had happened with Troy. And that dream. This one was the most real yet, just as real as the pavement beneath my feet. I grabbed my chest, feeling as if my heart was still split in two.

The thought of what Aphrodite had said sent shivers down my spine. My beloved had left me for Zeus. She was pregnant. My knees suddenly became weak.

In my dreams or visions, whichever they were, I had thought she loved me.

Have I completely lost it? Did I make up a life where I grew up on an island, my only companion a young woman who wore a hooded tunic and had eyes like the sea? Did I make up that conversation with Aphrodite? Did I imagine it all?

My chest still felt torn apart. Why did it all feel so real? "Why, Aphrodite?" I muttered. "Why end it all?"

I wanted so badly to go back to my dream and see if Aphrodite had done what I'd asked and sent me to my death. I wanted so badly to think I'd won the hooded woman's heart in the end. In the dreams, it *felt* like I had won. Every time I stared into her eyes, I felt love—beautiful and unconditional love. Her eyes were an energy source my spirit yearned for... breathed for. How I wished and longed for a love like that in my waking life.

If only love was as sweet as it is in my dreams.

Ashton claimed she saw love in my eyes for Taylor, which altered my perspective. I did feel something for Taylor. Not one day of summer had passed that I did not miss her terribly. But it was not the kind of love I felt in my dreams with the young woman, and not the kind I witnessed with Peitho and her Goddess.

I came up to a park near school and collapsed in the grass. The wind was mild and sweet, kissing my cheeks every time it blew. The sun was barely up, and already it was getting warm. I watched the colors shoot across the sky and had to smile. All the times I'd watched the sunset, I felt empty once the darkness conquered the light; yet I had forgotten it was just the opposite at sunrise, when light conquered the dark. I felt safe then, and so I drifted off to sleep.

Chapter 16

Remember

"Wake up," a voice said. "Petra, wake up."

The blinding sun burned my eyes. I saw through the light the silhouette of a man. He grabbed my arm and pulled me up to stand. Through his touch and skin, I sensed he deeply cared for me. Before my eyes could adjust, I thought it was Troy, but then I realized it was Ricky. The mistake made me realize just how similar the two of them looked.

"Ricky?" He was certainly the last person I'd expected. "What are you doing here?"

"Are you alright?" he asked.

I nodded, still surprised to see him.

"I saw you lying here unconscious and thought something must have happened to you."

"No, I fell asleep," I told him as I rubbed my eyes.

He gave me a sideways glance. "*Methysménos?*" he muttered, which means *drunk* in our language.

"What? No."

He nodded and smiled. "Are you heading back home?"

I nodded and started walking in that direction. He walked with me, watching me. I dragged my feet as slowly as I could; I had no desire to see Allison.

"Petra," he said suddenly, "I know we really haven't had a chance to talk about Tartarus and you saving me."

I quickly looked up at him just in time to see the solemnity in his eyes. I nodded and had to laugh. "Saving you? If you could even call it that."

"I suppose you're right," he said. "But I never thanked you either—for coming for me."

My feet dragged even more. "I know you would have done the same for me."

"Indeed. I would have."

We were quiet for some time as we kept walking. There was contentment in the silence, our steps on the street the only sound.

"Can I ask you a question?" I asked.

"Always."

"Who was the God you fell in love with to give you that?" I asked, pointing to his forearm where the Lambda brand was hidden under his long sleeves.

He wrapped his hand around it gently, as if it stung.

"Petra," he said earnestly. "What do you know about the Lambdas?"

My feet finally came to a halt. I gawked at him to let him know he'd insulted my intelligence. But I felt his concern, and soon my pride receded.

I focused on him with all the sincerity I had and admitted, "I guess I don't know very much at all."

"Then what have you been told?" he asked.

His question had me thinking back to what Dion had told me.

"Oh," I said, nodding my head, remembering, "they're called the Enlightened because they love who they love—either gender."

"Either gender," he said. "But you supposed it was the love of a God that earned me this brand?"

I nodded my head. "I-I assumed. Every Lambda I've met so far has been branded for falling in love with someone of their same gender." I paused. "It's why I'm banished…"

"That is only a branch of the full tree," he muttered. Then he turned to me and grabbed my shoulders gently. His eyes frightened me because they felt like they had hands of their own, grabbing my attention.

"Listen to me, Petra," he said, softly and slowly. "Listen to me carefully. We call the Lambdas the Enlightened. It is the enlightening that gives us the brand, not who we love. Finding your loved one is only the compass that directs you to the path of enlightenment. Because once we have found our true love, we have reunited with our counterpart—our soul mate. And therefore, we have begun to remember."

Remember. The word echoed in my head. *Remember.*

"Remember what?" I mumbled.

He stared at me for so long I thought his mind had gone somewhere else. Finally, he blinked a couple of times, as if coming back to the here and now.

"Petra, do you still have the charm bracelet I gave you when we were together?"

I flinched. It was such a random thing for him to ask. Yet, it took me back to the moment when Ricky gave me that chicken wire bracelet with a bronze myrtle charm on it. On the back of the charm, "13" was engraved. I remembered him jokingly, charmingly saying I was the thirteenth Olympian Goddess. That felt like a lifetime ago.

"Of course I do," I said, smiling. I kept it in my soccer bag.

"Good," he said.

I nodded, still confused, and ignored the severe weight I felt from him. We walked the rest of the way home in an electrifying silence.

When we arrived, I stood in front of the door for a minute before pushing it open with a sigh. Almost immediately, I felt Allison. *Great.* My nose scrunched with the stench, as if I'd smelled a rotten, decomposing corpse. Then I felt something else. My nose began to tingle, and tears started to form. Ashton was there, too.

They were sitting in the living room. We walked past them quickly and headed straight to my room. Then I heard someone gasp.

"What?" Allison asked under her breath.

I turned around just in time to see Allison's shocked face. She was standing up, staring at Ricky with heated eyes and clenched fists. I felt her extreme anger.

Ricky turned to her, and I wished I could see the look he was giving her. Allison remained staring, but Ashton acted as if he didn't exist.

"What the Hades was that about?" I asked once we were in my bedroom. I slammed the door behind me. Jaden slipped in seconds later.

"What's going on?" she asked.

"Ricky," I said, angrily. "Do you know Allison?"

"What happened?" Jaden asked.

Ricky ignored both of our questions. "Did Nick find it?" he asked Jaden. She nodded, "He's on his way."

"Good," he said, and then looked directly at me. "Get your charm bracelet." I didn't move, still shocked about Ricky's bizarre encounter with Allison.

He beckoned me again to get my charm bracelet. Finally, I went over to my closet and pulled my soccer bag down from the high shelf. Something fell out of it. My traveling scroll. The one I shared with Christy, Ann, and Chandra, my closest friends from Gaianus. Before I even bent to pick it up, Ricky snatched it and unrolled it.

"I can't believe it," he muttered. "Petra…"

"Ricky, that's nothing. It's just a scroll that I share with my friends." I tried to snatch it back from his hands, but he pulled away.

"Petra, we will definitely need this too."

My mouth dropped open to reply, but nothing came out.

Just then, Nick burst through the bedroom door.

"I got it!" he exclaimed, raising his arm. He was holding a lyre.

I had never seen a real lyre before, nor did I have the slightest idea how to play one. I had only seen a picture of one in a Gaianus book called *Attributes of Our Ancestors*. I remembered the lyre because it was an attribute of one of our most complex Olympian Gods, Apollo.

We'd spent half the time in class talking about his many gifts. He was the God of light and sun, truth and prophecy, healing, plague, poetry, and of course, music. The other half of class we talked about his attributes: the bow and arrow, his sacrificial tripod and his lyre. Thinking about that long day of class made me want to yawn.

Nick handed the lyre to Ricky.

"The charm bracelet?" Ricky asked. I reached into the side pocket of my soccer bag and felt it loop around my fingers. I pulled it out and took one good look at it before handing it to him.

"All that's left," he said, staring at me, "is the chest."

They all looked at me.

"The chest?" I asked, confused.

I moved my gaze across the room, meeting each of their eyes before finally settling in the corner of the bedroom where the archaic chest sat.

"Why do you want the chest?" I asked, still staring at it.

"It's time we open it, Petra," Ricky said.

"You found the key?" I asked. My voice felt far away.

"I think. But we can't do it here," he said.

"Let's go for a little drive then, shall we?" Nick asked, grinning.

We placed the traveling scroll in my soccer bag, along with the chest and lyre. As I shouldered the strap, we looked at each other once more before walking out of the bedroom.

Allison and Ashton hadn't moved from where we'd left them sitting on the couch. However, this time Allison didn't acknowledge Ricky when he walked past. They didn't even lift their heads at Nick and Jaden. It was only when I walked past that Allison raised her eyes to look at me. I felt pulled to a stop, and time slowed. Ashton didn't move a muscle, still focused on whatever paper she was reading. Allison looked at my soccer bag, and then she met my eyes. Her expression didn't change, but when I sensed her, she felt fearless, angry, and dark.

∞

We drove to a mountain ridge outside Regis. When the car stopped, the others got out quickly. I remained inside, looking out the window at the familiar forest.

"You coming, Petra?" Nick yelled. I opened the door, but before unbuckling and stepping out of the car, I sensed something different in the air. I shook it off, grabbed the soccer bag, and hopped out.

Ricky led us off the trail and into the thicker part of the woods. As we followed him, I started to recognize where he was leading us. He stopped close to where Ashton had brought me a couple months ago. As he bent down at the stream, cupped his hands full of water and took a sip, I shook off the memory of Ashton bathing in that stream. I walked over to Ricky and knelt down to sip the water. Then everything went dark.

I was falling.

∞

Finally, I landed near a river. It was pitch dark, the only light coming from the bottom of the river. The air smelled awful and foul, as if mold and death were all around me. My body crumbled next to the river, hands digging deeply into the banks of ash. I was crying, painfully, tears filling my swollen eyes. My mouth felt dry and my body weak and lifeless. I tried to speak, but my lips were too chapped and bloodied.

A gentle, glowing hand was suddenly around my waist. Then someone lifted my lifeless body into her glowing chest.

"Drink this," a beautiful voice said. "This will end it all."

I looked up from her bosom and saw her flawless hands holding the river water. I looked into her perfect face and glowing sapphire eyes and did what she told me. Then everything went white.

I jumped back from the stream. My foot caught on a rock and I fell back on my butt.

"What's wrong?" Ricky shouted as he stumbled trying to catch me.

"I-I saw—"

Nick and Jaden ran to me.

"What? What did you see?" Nick asked.

"I saw." I tried everything I could to catch my breath. "Aphrodite," I panted.

"What was it this time?" Jaden asked in a hurry.

"It was her," I said, exasperated. "She ended it… It was her?" I swallowed the knot in my throat. "She's the one who gave me water from Lethe. It had to be Lethe."

As I spoke, almost in unison, the three of them stood straight up and fell silent.

"Oh my gods," Jaden said, finally breaking the silence.

I looked at Ricky. He was staring out in the distance, into the trees, as if he'd gone somewhere in his thoughts and was not in the present moment.

I met eyes with Nick. His mouth hung open, and he was shaking his head in disbelief. All of us looked to him as if he knew what it all meant. I pleaded to the Gods for him to have the answer.

Finally, I caught my breath and stood up too.

Nick looked at Ricky. "Could it have been her?"

The question drew Ricky out of whatever train of thought he was on. He shook his head and then looked at us. "I don't know, but we need to hurry up and do this."

He grabbed the chest out of my soccer bag, gave it to Nick, and then reached for the scroll and handed it to Jaden. As she unrolled it, Ricky paused to look at the charm on the bracelet. He wore an unusual expression as he gawked at it for a while before reaching back into the bag for the lyre.

"Do you think this will really work?" Nick asked.

Ricky walked over to a thick pine near the stream and sat down against its trunk. He positioned himself so he could properly hold the lyre, leaning it against his leg and wrapping his fingers around its strings, similar to a harp. He looked up at Nick but didn't answer his question. Instead, he gave a hopeful smile as his fingers began to play a beautiful, soft, melancholy tune. Almost instantly, we all sat down and listened. I began to hum along.

I looked over at Jaden. Her face changed as she studied the scroll. So I scooted toward her, curious to know what she was seeing.

Jaden and I stared blankly as our jaws dropped. The scroll had begun to unveil charcoal writings underneath my friends' scribbled conversations.

We watched each word reveal itself as if a spirit were writing it.

The music Ricky was playing slowly started rising in harmony to something just as hopeful as the expression on his face. He didn't let up. And as the music began to rise in grace, the charcoal writing appeared more quickly.

Jaden started translating it from ancient Greek, singing aloud in English.

"A sweet angel came at sun's highest shine.
A guise she wore to hide some crime.
Young as I, though stunning as she,
my heart was blind, so could not see.

'O' Angel?' I call her by name,
though her tongue was not the same.
Instead, a smile was her reply.
My eyes saw trust and did comply.

Alas, at night, when full moon's bright,
she left me suddenly, tiptoeing light.
Quick as I learnt, the quicker she would leave.
I learnt to sit still with myself to grieve.

Until thy light comes soon again,
I wait for a moonless night to ascend.
Hither and thither she comes like the breeze.
Though what she dost not know,
will make her fall to her knees.

I thought it then, but know it now,
love hid all this time behind a cloud.
I loved young and once before,
though in this life it's been barely a score.

I will feel that heart more than twice.
Our souls will not go far, but will splice.
The sea in her eyes, and my name in her heart,
forever our love could never impart."

The singing suddenly stopped, as did the music. We all sat around looking at one another as if something had become clear, though I was still as confused as ever. Although the self-written poem was the reason for my confusion, that it was on my traveling scroll irritated me more.

Jaden softly touched my wrist, turned it, and then let go. "Are you okay?"

"Yeah," I said, perplexed. I didn't understand her question. Was the poem supposed to wound me somehow? Was it supposed to affect me?

"Try to remember," Ricky said. His words vibrated through my ears.

Remember...? Remember what?

Poseidon had demanded the same thing before showing me Peitho and her Goddess. I hadn't known what Poseidon was talking about then, and I didn't know what Ricky was talking about now. How could I remember something if I didn't even know what to remember? I was growing frustrated.

I grabbed the scroll from Jaden's hands and looked at the charcoal writing. It was in the poorest penmanship, very old writing, and in our ancient tongue. I couldn't understand a thing. Some words were familiar from classes at Gaianus, but most words were unrecognizable. The one word that stood out was *agape*. I traced my fingers over the ancient word.

There was a bright white flash.

I was holding a stick of charcoal, writing the word *agape*. I looked up and saw her eyes smile. I wished I could see her lips.

Then time shot me back to the present. I was still holding the scroll, my finger still on the word. I shook my head and blinked a couple of times, trying to focus on the word.

"Can you read any of it?" Ricky asked.

I looked at the five cryptic stanzas once more and started trying to sound out each word using the little I'd learned at Gaianus. My tongue tripped on each word horribly, but soon I found a decent flow. As I read the second line, my head started to get very heavy, and my ears began to ring. I tried to ignore it and kept reading.

As each word flowed through my tongue, my forehead felt like it was protruding out, throbbing painfully, and the ringing grew even louder. I pinched my forehead, trying to relieve the pain, but when I did, white filled my eyes.

Another flash. My hand holding the charcoal stick, writing the ancient poem. My voice, speaking the ancient tongue perfectly, as if I had known it my whole life, with such fluidity and eloquence. My hand, writing the words down in the past as I spoke them aloud in the present time.

I saw the fire and waves crashing behind her. Her white hood covering her face, the darkness obscuring everything but her eyes. Her tunic falling loosely over her flawless skin. Her beautiful hands glowing with warmth. Her gentle fingers playing with her necklace.

I got to the last line and closed my eyes, then opened them to see my bronze charm hanging on her necklace, tangled in her fingers. I recognized the myrtle shape and the "13" embossed on the back. I gasped. It felt as if the pressure in my head had finally exploded, like whatever was blocking this memory had been destroyed. I was lightheaded and dizzy.

"The bracelet," I said softly.

Ricky handed it to me without hesitation.

I took it in my hand and looked at it. One tear fell into my palm. I turned to Nick, who was holding the chest. I took it from his hands, placed it on the ground, and looked at it with a smile. I then put the bronze myrtle charm into one of the bronze locks. It snapped open. I did the same thing to the other lock and it snapped open as well.

We all let out a breath as I lifted the chest's lid.

Chapter 17

The Angel

Every memory came at me in a burst of light.

I was alone on the island with my youngest older brother. My other two brothers had had to leave with my mother and father. They'd had to go to the mainland to get more resources for our family. My father had told us not to worry, for the angels and mermaids of the island would protect us. My father was convinced they were watching over us, but I had never seen one.

Until the day my youngest brother disappeared.

My brother and I had been on the island alone for a few lunar years, and he had found a hobby. A clever way to make liquor out of the myrtle that grew freely on the island. He called it Mirto. I never asked him how he learned to make it or where he thought of the name. Making it made him happy. That was all I cared about. I rarely saw him throughout the day, and he would come back late, smelling of it. I hated the smell. It was bitter and foul.

One day, when the sun was high in the sky, I spotted my first mermaid. I sat on the grassy knoll under a crooked palm tree, staring out to sea until nightfall. I counted three mermaids total. I did not call for them, shout, or even move from my spot; I just watched. They swam back and forth near a set of rocks on the shore, and then back into the sea. They were the most beautiful creatures I had ever seen, and for once, I believed my father; I believed they were protecting me.

I woke up the next morning on the grassy knoll and went back up the stream to our home in the cave. There was no sign of my brother. That was when I became frightened.

I searched the island for days, losing count of how many times the sun rose and set. I stopped for food and water but had no time for sleep. If I woke up to find myself on the floor, I would get up and begin searching again. I searched endlessly, tediously, but there was no sign of him. Finally, after several moon cycles, I stopped searching and forced myself to admit that he was gone. I blamed his disappearance on the mermaids, and for a long time I thought they had taken him.

It was a while before I decided to leave our home in the cave and set up camp where my brother used to make his Mirto. The smell I'd once hated became a smell I loved. I felt his warmth every time I smelled it, and I would fall asleep wishing it was him coming home after a long night of fermenting. I missed him terribly, painfully, even more than I missed the rest of my family.

He'd been the last family I had left.

More time passed and there was still no sign of my family or any other human on the island. Then one day, I woke up to an angel. I knew she was an angel because her skin glowed like the moon. She wore a white tunic with a hood that hid every part of her face, except her eyes. Although I could not see her face, I still found her strangely beautiful and couldn't help looking at her.

"What's your name?" I asked.

She looked at me, and without responding, started walking to the sea. I thought she must be one of the mermaids I'd seen so long ago and became angry at her almost immediately. However, when she stepped into the water, her feet did not change into fins. She walked further into the sea, to a small wooden dock I had never seen before.

Tied to the dock was a tiny fishing boat. She pointed to it, and then looked at me, touched her chest, and pointed to the ground. She then pointed to the waning crescent moon and waved her hands back and forth. I realized what she was saying: she would come when there was no moon—a new moon. I nodded to her and smiled. She came back over to me and knelt to meet my eyes.

The first time I saw her eyes, they shone just as brightly as the sea behind her. I stared into them and saw the light of creation and all its beauty. I was completely in awe. For the first time since my brother disappeared, I felt warmth. Her eyes had restored all the life I'd lost that day.

She seemed to be searching for words, thinking hard about what to say. When she finally spoke hesitantly, I didn't understand her. It was a tongue unfamiliar to my ears. I shook my head.

Her eyes grew sad beneath the darkness of her hood, and I felt sad too.

"How old are you?" she asked, in my own tongue. It was broken, but coming from her lips still sounded beautiful.

I shrugged and put up several fingers, then all ten of them. It was my best guess.

"Where are your mom and dad?" she asked, and then smiled with her eyes.

I didn't know the answer. It had been several lunar cycles since I'd last seen them, and the memory of the day they left made me sadder than before.

"Deceased," I said, and then shrugged again.

Her eyes frowned. She then grabbed me and tucked me into her body.

The angel held me as if I were her child. As she held me close to her chest, I listened to her heart beating. It was at that moment that I suddenly realized I would never see my mother, father, and three brothers ever again. I began to weep into her bosom.

It was the first time I'd cried for my family, and I had never cried so hard in my life. I cried myself to exhaustion, and when I woke up, it was night. The angel had lit a fire and caught some fish. She pulled a dagger from the belt on her tunic and set it on the ground. It was shiny and beautiful, better than the makeshift knife I'd made from twine and a rock that I'd sharpened into a point. The hilt was white marble with gold accent lines on the sides, and the blade was silver and sparkled in the firelight.

I eyed the angel's mystic beauty in silence as she took one of the fish in both of her hands, closed her eyes, and began mumbling words I didn't understand. When she was finished, she took her dagger and slit the fish's chin, all the way down to its belly, releasing its guts and head into the fire pit. I felt nauseated. She placed its body on a smooth rock sitting at the edge of the fire, and then did the same with the other fish.

I had never eaten fish before. My family and I ate what the land gave us, not the sea. My father had once told us that we should never take from the sea, for everything in the sea belonged to Poseidon.

"What is your name?" the angel asked, breaking the silence.

I touched my chest in question. I had almost forgotten who I was. I had not heard my name spoken out loud in a very, very long time—had begun to believe I never would need one again.

"Sappho," I said. "And yours?"

Her eyes glowed through the fire as I waited for her answer.

"Leto," she replied softly.

"Leto," I said smiling. "Are you an angel?"

She paused and watched me, her glowing eyes pinched in on the sides. "I am no angel," she said finally, "but I am not like you either."

"I see," I lied. I did not see. I was quiet for a long moment. "Then who are you like?" I finally asked.

I thought I heard her giggle as she pointed to a cluster of stars. "My people come from there, in the constellation of Taurus."

She looked at me through the fire as she flipped the fish over on the rock.

"Taurus," I repeated. "What is a con-constellation?"

She grabbed a stick and began poking at the embers. "A constellation is an alliance of stars in the Heavens."

"You're from the Heavens?" I asked, slightly thrilled.

She stopped poking and looked up at me. Her eyes were wide and she nodded. "I am."

"You're a Goddess?"

"I suppose," she said quietly.

My heart started beating excitedly. Yet I was confused. "I've never heard of the Goddess Leto."

She did not speak, just sat and looked at her fish. I leaned down to try to look into her eyes. The hood covered her very well, but as her eyes glowed brightly, I could still see their sadness.

"Eat your fish before it goes cold," she said gently.

I looked down at my fish but had no appetite for it. Even after so many seasons without hearing my father's words, I was reluctant to disobey what he'd told me about eating from Poseidon's sea.

"Poseidon is the God of the Sea," my father would say, *"and he will take care of us if we obey him."*

"Do you know Poseidon?" I asked.

Leto set her empty leaf down near the fire. "Yes," she said. "He is my favorite cousin."

My jaw dropped, as did my fish.

She reached through the fire and grabbed my fish, now covered in sand. She wiped it with her white tunic, and then placed it back on my leaf.

"He is the one who told me you were here," she said.

∞

After that night by the campfire, she came every new moon, just as she'd said, and left every full moon. Every time she came, she taught me about the other Gods of her kind and about our mother Earth, Gaia. Every time she left, it was as if the sun left with her, leaving me in the dark.

She woke me up very early one day, before dawn, and gave me a bow and a quiver full of arrows.

"Today I will teach you how to hunt."

"But I already know how," I protested, pulling my makeshift dagger from my belt.

She laughed and grabbed my hand, pulling me up to stand.

"No wonder you're so skinny," she quipped.

Offended, I grabbed the bow and quiver and stomped into the woods.

"Skinny girl has a temper, too," she said, following behind me.

"I have hunted many moon cycles by myself," I called back to her.

"Sappho, remember we go by a Lunisolar cycle—twelve lunar months and three hundred and fifty-four days."

"Fine," I said, exasperated. "I have hunted over two thousand days by myself, with just my dagger. I do not need a hunting lesson."

I stopped abruptly and turned around to face her. She was treading lightly behind me, carrying our packs, and of course, still wearing her hood.

"And how can you hunt with your hood on?" I snapped.

She stopped walking and her eyes pinched in with anger. I was glad to see it. This whole year, she had been the perfect angel, always nice and teaching me with perfect patience. She was a stone, and I wanted a reaction.

"You always wear it. When you sleep, when you bathe, even on the hottest of days. Why, Leto? When can I see your face and fully see this angel who has cared for me?"

She gave no hint of reply, which made me even angrier.

"Take it off!" I shouted.

"No, my child," she said gently.

"Leto, I beg you, let me see you."

"No, Sappho." She was still perfectly, annoyingly calm. "Stop this."

"Leto, please! Just once," I pleaded.

"No, I can't!"

"But *why* can you not?"

She said nothing.

"Why?" I shouted.

She still didn't respond.

"Take it off, Leto!" I yelled, reaching for her hood. "Take it off—"

"I'm an exile!" she cried out, finally.

I stopped reaching. I had no response. I didn't know what an exile was, but it didn't sound very good. I looked at her, confused.

"I am in hiding, my child." She gasped, as if it pained her to say it aloud.

"Hiding?" I asked softly. "From what?"

"From some very bad beings," she muttered, and then walked past me.

I realized then that it was wrong for me to want to see her angry, and I didn't want to see her in pain. I didn't ask her about it again.

∞

Two years passed. Today was my thirteenth birthday, and Leto had lit a fire with just a rock and tinder. It always impressed me how she could start a fire from anything available.

As she built up the fire, I stared into the night sky. "Where is it I come from?" I asked aloud.

She didn't respond as she fed the fire a bit of wood and some brush, barely enough for any light or warmth.

"That is not enough wood, don't you think?" I asked.

She shook her head. "Tonight, I am teaching you about the Heavens."

She didn't have to look up; she already knew I was smiling. I had been begging her to teach me about the constellations for years. She would always say, "not until you're old enough," and today I was old enough.

"Get your scroll and your charcoal stick and try to write down what I say."

My smile grew even bigger. Earlier that day, when she'd first arrived, she had gifted me fresh new scrolls and charcoal already carved into a thick stick for writing. My favorite thing to do was to write. Although my penmanship was horrible, Leto assured me it would get better in time.

I went into my leather pack, grabbed one of the finely rolled papyrus scrolls, and dug deeply for the charcoal stick. I set myself against a log and reclined back, getting comfortable for the teachings.

Leto's eyes pinched into a smile. She pointed to the southern part of the sky above her head. "Do you see those three stars, slightly apart from each other though forming a line?"

I nodded.

"That is called Orion's belt, of the constellation Orion. Your kind calls it the Hunter."

I drew a diagram of the stars and quickly wrote down what she said, word for word. As soon as I was done, I looked back up at her, excitedly.

She pointed again. "And those stars there, south from the Hunter, are called the Lepus, or the Hare." She turned to me and her eyes pinched in again. "The Hunter chases the Hare."

I laughed and looked back up at the Heavens. "Look, there's Taurus," I said, pointing.

She nodded. "Very good, Sappho."

But she sounded sad. I tried to figure out why, and then remembered three years ago when she'd told me her people were from Taurus.

"When you leave every full moon, do you go back home?" I asked.

She was surprised at my question and did not answer for a long time.

"No," she said curtly. And without another word, she stood up and walked down to the shoreline.

∞

I was twenty years old now and had grown into a woman. And since sixteen, my love for her had grown as well. Now that I was older, we spent our time in games and conversation. Today she decided we would play a game of tag. I joked we were well over the age for such games, but she persisted, and then held up two bottles of Mirto while giggling.

"We will see who can hold her liquor this time."

She was referring to the last game of tag we'd played. I had added a rule that every time someone got tagged they would take a drink of my brother's Mirto. It was not a very long game; I ended up having too much too fast.

I took a big gulp of Mirto before chasing after her. The ten-year-old wine was absolutely delicious, and our favorite thing to reward ourselves with after a day of hunting and chores at the conservatory we'd built over the years. I wished I could tell my brother that he was an excellent wine maker.

We were soon on our third bottle, but I was pacing myself better this time. I chased her onto the beach. I could smell the liquor pouring from her skin as I ran behind her. We reached the shoreline near the water. I planned to tackle her into the sea, but she was too quick. She splashed me teasingly and then made a run for it up onto the softer sand.

I will never forget what happened next.

As I turned around to watch her run, a big gust of wind came from the north shore. It was then, before I blinked, that her hood fell off her head and onto her shoulders. For the first time in ten years, her golden hair was freed.

My feet stopped moving, the gracious gust of wind stopped blowing, and for a moment, my heart stopped beating. It was just the back of her head, but in that moment, my world froze. In slow motion, she turned toward me. I caught a glimpse of her cheek and gasped. Something tugged at my heart as she kept turning and the side of her lips came into view.

This is it.

My stomach ached for this moment.

But before she finished turning, she noticed her hood and quickly pulled it back over her head. My hope disappeared.

Since I'd realized I was in love with her four years ago, that hood had haunted my dreams every night. It was the one thing keeping us apart, keeping me from fully knowing her. I hated it with all of my being. Was she never going to let me in?

When she faced me once more, she had pulled the hood so far down that I couldn't even see her eyes anymore. That was when I began to cry.

"What is it?" she asked softly, moving quickly toward me.

My lips began to tremble. I didn't need to see her eyes to know that she saw them; she stepped closer and reached out to caress my cheek.

Her touch made me hurt more. I couldn't speak, and my lips began to tremble harder. Gently, she brushed her thumb against them. That was something she had never done before. I felt weak but tried to deny it as I watched the colors of twilight shoot across the sky. Her fingers gently brushed even more softly against my trembling lips once more, and then moved toward my chin. Her touch was so gentle. I wanted to melt into her.

146

I felt my walls begin to splinter. I needed her. Now. I needed to see her. No hood—no more hiding.

I reached into the darkness of her hood to touch her. I had never attempted it before, and I expected her to move away. When she didn't, my hand came upon her cheek. As soon as my fingers pressed against her skin, sorrow filled my heart, for I would never see the cheek I was holding. My thumb brushed her lips, and I nearly cried, for nor would I ever see the smile those lips created. I took in what I was touching. It was a texture I had never felt before, soft and warm, but at the same time cold and hard.

"A cold stone couldn't give me so much warmth," I muttered.

I felt her skin scrunch into a smile beneath my palm.

"Can I have you now?" I asked in a whisper that held all the sincerity my heart carried.

She didn't move, but her smile vanished. There was a long silence as I choked on her unspoken words. She then turned around and walked away, leaving me holding empty air. As my hand fell back to my side, my heart fell to the ground. I didn't want her to see that she had hurt me, so I turned around and allowed the sea to sting my eyes. The waves were crashing hard into the rocks, and the tide crawled higher onto the shore. The waves were a perfect reflection of my pain.

But then, a hand on my shoulder gently turned me around. All I saw was darkness before I felt her soft lips on mine.

I had never imagined this kiss could happen. Yet there we stood, lips pressed tightly together. The sun began to set as the tide grew higher, creeping between our toes. Our walls had finally shattered, my glass and her stone falling between us onto the sand, letting the waves carry them away.

She let go quickly, her eyes wild with surprise. I didn't know what to think and didn't have time to before she rushed at me again. Her lips pressed harder into mine this time, with urgency and fire. She released me and we both panted for air, and then she went in again, lips and tongues fighting to taste and touch.

We dropped to the ground as the tide splashed over us. I dug my fingers into the sand and pressed my body into hers. She let out a soft moan. Our kisses were passionate, heated. I pushed myself up to give us a breath, and then I saw it. Her hood lay in the sand. I could finally see her face, the light from the nearly full moon lighting it well. I loved the moon that enabled me to see every perfect line and dimple. Fair, pale skin. Those almond-shaped eyes the color of the sea. Two pronounced dimples pinched in her cheeks as she smiled softly. She had the most adorable chin, proud, round, and strong. Her lips were pink and full. She was beautiful. Perfect. And immortal.

Quickly, almost too quickly, the thought surfaced: *Why would she ever want me?*

Her smile slowly faded as she stared up at me in question. I leaned down and kissed her with a kiss that said, *Thank you.*

"You are so beautiful," I whispered between soft kisses, and felt her lips curl up in a smile.

I wanted to do so much to her, touch every part of her body with my lips, give her all the love I'd had pent up inside me for so many years. But I had no clue what to do with the want I felt. I had never done this before. This was one thing Leto had left out of my teachings. Still, within me, I felt my body somehow already knew what to do. But before touching her, before showing her how much I loved her, I needed to tell her. I needed to finally say the words that had been on the tip of my lips for years.

"*Écho agapísei*," I whispered. There was no other way to put it. I had loved her "for a long time." I hesitated. "It has been hard to understand it all."

She said nothing. I thought her eyes glistened, but it must have only been the moonlight.

I placed my fingers on the collar of her tunic. It was soaked from the tide, yet warm from her body. Her eyes stayed on me, lips apart, drinking in the air. My fingers dragged down the collar of the tunic, down her chest, down to the belt tie. Then I stopped. She was trembling.

"Are you cold?" I asked.

I felt her chest rise against mine, and then fall. Rise, and then fall... rise, and then fall. Every inhale pulled at my top lip, and every exhale pushed at my bottom one. No words came out of her, only quick pants of breath. Fear began to creep into my mind. Was I scaring her? Slowly, I began to get up, but she stopped me.

"N-no," she said, though her lips still trembled.

"What is it you want?" I asked.

She closed her eyes. I felt her disappear from me then. I had said the wrong thing.

Her eyes slowly opened, and her hand reached out to touch my chest with a flat palm. I looked down at her hand, over my heart, and then back down at her. This time there was no question; her eyes were glistening with tears.

Very slowly, I leaned over her, reached for her cheek with my fingertips, and kissed her. Her lips took form with mine as if forged from the same fire, holding all the same desire, and sending shivers all over my body. It was soft as a feather and sweet as a summer rain.

She placed her hand on top of mine and kissed my fingers gently. Her eyes held mine for a beautiful second, and then slowly she started moving my hand down her body and onto her belt tie. Her fingers moved mine, and with little effort, the tie was undone, and her tunic fell open.

I had never experienced such nerves. I couldn't move. Perhaps I was in shock. Never in my wildest, sweetest dreams had I ever thought this could be possible.

I no longer needed the moonlight to see, for she glowed even brighter than the moon. Her body destroyed every definition of perfect. My hands shook and my lips trembled as her arms brought me into her chest, and I fell onto her bare-stone skin. Her heart thumped against my ear. I closed my eyes and allowed myself to get lost in her sound. I was safe, my body warm. Nothing had ever felt more right.

My fingers traced the bottom of her breast, and the thumping of her heart quickened. I watched her breast lift into the night sky and then fall back down to Earth as she breathed. My fingers gently traced around her nipple, which lifted with sharpened poise, and I watched it react to my touch before kissing it with my lips. I moved my fingers down to her navel and rested them there. Her stomach tightened at my touch and she inhaled another deep breath. I liked the reaction, so I traced my finger along her hips and back up to her navel. Her stomach tightened harder, though this time no breath drew in. I lifted my head and saw her eyes closed, her face peaceful.

I watched her as I continued my curious journey from her hip down to her inner thigh. She squirmed, and I stopped and waited for her to catch up with my desire. I dragged my fingers further down her inner thigh and then back up, until finally neither of us could take it any longer.

Our lips met and our bodies began to move in a slow, unified motion, as if we had done this dance numerous times even though it was our first. Her hands felt me everywhere. She knew the paths of my body, which roads to take, where to touch and when to wait. My body responded to her every touch. She had control over me, and I didn't care. I didn't want her to stop.

And then she dove into me. One touch and I began to float into space. My body arched, kissing the stars. I felt myself falling away from her, my fingers slipping off her. She dove in further, opening me up. I felt my spirit leave me. I reached for her then, but the desire was building too fast, making me lose focus, forget what I was doing, until I couldn't take it anymore. I let out a gasping moan and felt the ghost of me leave my body. Pleasure's hands cradled me, spoke to me sweetly, kissed me gently, filling my body with life. My ghost fell back into my body. I sucked in a breath, and then sank into her embrace.

Was it real? Could a feeling such as this exist? I hadn't known. Life had given me many gifts, but never one such as this. What made this gift even sweeter was that it had come from her touch, from her kiss. I wanted her to be in this ecstasy with me. I wanted her forever in it with me.

My hands resumed the journey they'd started earlier. I wanted to discover every bit of her. Her desire poured out as I parted her legs with my thigh, and she bit down on her bottom lip as my fingers parted the folds between her legs. I went into her, into the damp darkness with a confidence that surprised me. I shined my curious light on the unknown and sparked a flame within her. I moved the light and watched her dance, awed at the discoveries I made. As I continued with curiosity, her dance quickened against me.

Our chests pressed together, and I dove in deeper. She began to cry out softly, moaning into my ear, and then lifting into me. I pressed down into her and felt her hips pump with mine. She wanted to do this together. Her body moved under me and she began to caress me. Her eyes glowed with the moon; I wanted her to see me and the pleasure she caused.

She held her breath. The fire was brightly burning now, her desire uncontrollable. I pressed into her more, and her hips pressed harder into mine. Her mouth burst with a breath as she cried out a sound that made my heart go crazy. Her hips collapsed into the wet sand and I buried my head in her shoulder, breathing in her celestial scent of jasmine and the sea. I took one last deep breath and lifted my head to look at her. There were tears in her eyes. I reached for her cheek, marveling at her beauty.

The light had discovered everything, and for the first time, I saw all of her. She had let me in. My own tears started to fall on her flawless, pale skin, untouched by the sun. I bent down gently to kiss her smile.

∞

The next morning, she woke me with a soft kiss. The fresh scent of jasmine and lavender blew across my nose, immediately warming me. I opened my eyes and saw the dark silhouette of a hood.

I sat up quickly. "Why?"

"I have to go, Sappho." She put her hand on my chest, over my heart, and began to cry. "Please don't make this any harder."

"No, please. Don't leave."

"I have to," she said.

As she stood up, her hand lifted off my chest. I felt it then. My heart was no longer there. It was gone—leaving with her.

Chapter 18

Letters to Aphrodite

A flash of light swallowed me up and dropped me back in front of Nick, Jaden, Ricky, and the open chest.

The four of us gazed into it. I saw the ancient chest open and couldn't help but feel as if my own chest was too. As if this chest were the key, I finally realized where my heart had gone. It was in the hands of the Goddess Leto.

"That's it?" Nick said. "Scrolls?"

"What are these?" Jaden asked.

"Sappho's poems," I said softly. "*My* poems."

Poseidon was right. This chest had been mine for centuries. Leto had given it to me on my seventeenth birthday, after seeing my scrolls all piled in a corner. I wish I'd known what she was thinking as she stared at the pile.

"There are so many," I remembered her saying. *"What did you need to say so much?"*

The truth, and what Leto did not know, was that after realizing I loved her, I'd begun writing to Aphrodite. And hadn't stopped until the day she'd left me forever.

I locked eyes with Ricky, who had the ghost of a smile on his face. He reached into the chest and took out a scroll. The rest of us followed suit, each grabbing one of our own to read. I unrolled mine and smiled.

O' undying Aphrodite,
daughter of high Ouranos,
I pray to you,
tame not my soul with heavy woe,
nor with anguish!

But please come,
if you are so inclined, and listen to my crying,
from your father's palace down descending

over dark earth
through middle ether
down from the heaven.

Come, my goddess.
With smiling, undying eyes, you ask,
What was the woe that troubled me?
What thing di I long for to appease my frantic
Soul: and whom now must I persuade?

Come to me now, my Aphrodite
And from tyrannous sorrow free me,
And all things my soul desires to have done,
Do for me, and let yourself be my great ally!

I remembered writing it like it was yesterday. I was sixteen and discovering the feeling of being in love with someone for the first time. Leto had left a couple of days before, and I hadn't known what to do with this new emotion for her, so I'd written to the only person I knew who would help me understand: Aphrodite, the Goddess of Love. I'd never thought Aphrodite would hear me, but she had. When I saw her, her beauty frightened me. I had never seen that kind of beauty before, and I didn't think I was even worthy of seeing it. She was very kind to me that day; she was always very kind to me.

Ricky looked up from the scroll he was reading. His eyes pinched in and for a second, I didn't know if he was smiling or squinting at me. I put my scroll back in the chest and reached in for another one.

My Goddess, fear you not,
I know the time when love's arms come into mine
Therefore, my sonnets of woes and love are no more,
My Goddess has come and assured:

Gild-glory, learnt from my heart.
Persuaded and sure, my embraced has come ashore
and my Goddess thus to be grateful for.

Alas, farewell, my celestial dove.
Chorus the sky sings.
I am within love's stronghold,
Sweet embraced arms of my beloved Leto.

This hymn was written the morning after Leto and I made love, and I'd told Aphrodite I finally had my beloved's heart, and therefore would not need her counsel any longer. It was my goodbye letter to her. The last letter I ever wrote her.

I shook my head slowly, feeling my heart breaking all over again. I slowly put my fingertips on my chest as ancient thoughts flooded my head of the days after I'd realized that Leto would not be returning to me. I felt betrayed all over again. By Leto. By love.

I wasn't deserving of her.

Sappho's memories and emotions whirled around my head and heart. What a fool I had been. She never could have truly loved me. I was just Sappho. A mortal. I could feel everything Sappho—everything *I* had felt, again. And suddenly I prayed I could not feel again. I prayed to not remember.

I don't want to remember.

"I know why she did it," I said in a whisper.

Jaden and Nick looked up from their scrolls.

"Who?" Jaden asked.

"Did what?" Nick said.

"Aphrodite. I know why Aphrodite brought me to Lethe. Sappho told Aphrodite to end it," I said, repeating the words I now remembered saying.

"Leto played me for a fool," I muttered to myself. "She was never an exile; she was only hiding her heart from Zeus. Zeus was who she loved." *Never me.* "He was always the one she would go back to." I gasped at the realization. "She never loved me."

My head and chest were throbbing. I was beginning to unravel. My limbs felt weak, and I could barely hold myself up. A thousand-year-old betrayal was hurting me as if it had just happened in this exact moment. I looked at Jaden and Nick, barely able to make out their expressions because tears began to well up in my eyes.

"But Aphrodite did," I said.

Ricky looked up and immediately I sensed his pain and sympathy.

"Aphrodite gave me another life. A better one," I continued. "She must have taken me to the river Lethe, given me the water to sip from her hands, to help me forget Leto." I paused and started shaking my head. "I should be grateful to Aphrodite. She carried my soul into a better life—as an immortal."

I stopped as the vision of me lying in Aphrodite's arms came as clear as day. Suddenly, my chest began to burn under the skin.

"She was the one who made me into Petra," I said. "The Goddess of Emotion; the Goddess who can feel everyone's heart but her own." I stared at each of their faces. "Aphrodite saved Sappho—she saved me."

Chapter 19

The Unveiling

"No," Ricky said softly. His eyes surprisingly carried the sun's warmth in them. "Aphrodite lied to you," he said sternly. "Leto *was* in exile."

My head shook; I didn't want to believe him. In my mind, I'd found the answer and there was no way of telling me otherwise. I had already begun hating Leto all over again for making a fool of me.

"She was hiding from Zeus," he continued.

I shook my head vigorously. "That was all a lie. How can I know that's true? For the Gods' sake, she was pregnant with his child. How could she be pregnant with his child if she didn't love him?" I shouted, then sighed. "She loved him…"

A stabbing burn ached at my chest again, feeling as if a slow burn fire was in the place where my heart should be. I didn't realize my head was still shaking until Ricky stepped up to me and placed his hands on either side of my face to stop my head from moving. His hands were gentle and held so much warmth. He stared into my eyes.

"She was scared to love, but it was not him she was scared of loving." He stepped even closer, closing the gap between us, and brought my face closer to his. "Petra," he continued, "listen to me. Shortly after the last day you saw her, she was captured."

He looked down, as if trying to find the words he needed to say. "Petra," he muttered, then lifted his head slowly and met my gaze. Pain. I could feel his sadness. "It was Aphrodite who captured Leto and brought her to Zeus."

Suddenly, something happened. We heard it before we saw it. Before I could even react to what Ricky had told me, his eyes went wide, then confused. He choked, and coughed up blood. Warm dots of blood splattered across my face. We both gasped and at the same time, looked down at the arrow coming out of his stomach, poking between our midriffs. I stepped back in shock. Suddenly the arrowhead split into grapnels. In that instant, our eyes met again, and this time there was no sadness or confusion but hope. Vindication.

The grapnels dug deeper into his skin, and in a blink of an eye, his body tore away from mine and into the darkness of the woods.

"Ricky!" I screamed.

War cries called out from the trees. Though we couldn't see them, I could feel who our attackers were. I had felt them before near Tartarus. The Heavens' Guards were back to get what was taken from them.

Within seconds, they came pushing through the trees and splashing angrily across the river. This time they wore bright gold armor, embellished with the seal of Zeus. They held weaponry built from the Gods' finest titanium. They looked like giants coming to slaughter lambs.

They stopped, and I counted off a dozen as they stood before us, clearly waiting for something. My eyes found the chest a few feet away from me, the charm still stuck in the lock. I dove for the chest, but one of the guards stomped his foot down in front of me before I reached it, knocking it on its side. Suddenly the guards parted their line in the middle, and out from where they split stepped three creatures.

Jaden held onto me as the beautiful creatures approached us. I looked back at the chest; the charm had dropped from the lock and into the dirt. The three creatures wore hooded maroon robes entwined with gold and black vines and flowers. Simultaneously, the three lifted off their hoods and unveiled themselves before us. I recognized them immediately. They were exactly how Allison had described them to me the past spring. The Guardians of Time. The Horai.

One of them pointed at Nick. Instantly, Jaden and I knew what they wanted, and we cried out for him. A vine shot from one of their sleeves and sprung out toward Nick, as a snake would attack its prey. The vine twisted around his wrist like chains. The Horai tugged hard at the vine, pulling him forward until he landed near her feet. She didn't even look at him when doing this, but held her gaze on Jaden and me.

Finally, I met each of their gazes, and instantly could feel myself being mesmerized by their beauty. After what they had done by taking my friends away, I still couldn't feel any hatred toward them. I must have been under their enchantments. They were too beautiful to hate.

They didn't look like they had skin because their glow was so bright, translucent even. Each one of them had the same piercing white-gold eyes and long flowing hair, but in different colors. One had red curls, the tallest had thick, dark tresses, and the youngest had curly golden locks.

"Now is not the time to go saving lives, Petra," the brunette hissed. I imagined she was the oldest, Eunomia, the Sister of Good Order.

"Especially those who are punished," the golden-haired sister said lightly with a smile. Eirene, the Sister of Peace.

Jaden squeezed my hand tightly. My mouth was dry and chalky. I could only nod my head. My eyes quickly shot to Nick, who was lying at the last sister's feet. The redhead, who I gathered would be Dike, the Sister of Justice. She looked at me awry as Nick held my gaze with shame.

"Do it again, and you'll be next," Eunomia said sharply.

Each of them gave me a distinct look before turning back to the forest; Dike a dangerous glare, Eirene a polite smile, and Eunomia a solemn expression with a curious raise of the eyebrow.

The gold-armored guards soon followed them, stomping behind as they pulled Nick along with them. I rushed over to the chest and collapsed on it. At least the chest and Jaden were safe. Once they left, there was silence. It was as if they had never come and taken my two friends. My chest began to burn again and I wanted to cry.

"Damnit!"

Jaden and I stared at each other for a long second, not knowing what to say. This was all my fault. Ricky and Nick just wanted to help me find who I was, and now they would both be punished for it. While I was left unpunished, left with my chest burning. I needed to get them back. I didn't know if it was the guilt, or the overwhelming desire to save people, but I knew without hesitation what I needed to do. And I could care less about the Horai's warning.

I looked back into the haunting trees that Ricky and Nick had disappeared into.

Fuck them.

"I'm going to get them back," I said aloud, breaking the eerie silence of the forest. "I don't know how, but I will."

∞

Jaden looked at me from across the room. "I don't know what to do," she mumbled.

Neither do I.

158

I sat quietly, threading a string through the myrtle charm. Once threaded, I tied it around my neck.

I knew why they'd taken Ricky. They were taking him back to Tartarus. But I didn't understand why they were punishing Nick, the Messenger God, and not me. Why would the Horai punish the accomplice and not the criminal?

I started thinking about the reasons they'd banished Ricky in the first place, and what Ricky had said came rushing to my head. *"It's the enlightening that gives us the brand, not who we love."*

My mind tore in two as I remembered why Allison's branding had occurred. She'd said it was all because of love. If it wasn't *who* they loved that gave them the brand, then what was the enlightenment the Lambdas had received? I was stuck with those questions, praying for answers. What was the enlightenment? And what *choice* did Ricky make to get himself banished to Tartarus?

I didn't feel hurt, or angry, or vengeful. All I felt was tired. The flash of hope I'd seen in Ricky's eyes kept replaying in my mind. My head was heavy, my eyes puffy, and my body felt like it didn't belong to me.

Beauty and fear were what I saw in the abyss. There was something unreal about the time on the clock, the bed beneath me, and the presence of Jaden in front of me. Time and space, which had seemed so far apart and expanded, were now compacting into one solid motion. My soul was continuous, and it had lived another life before. And in that life, before this one, I was a mortal, a student, a poet... I was Sappho.

I remembered Ricky's words once more. *"Finding your loved one is only the compass that directs you to the path of enlightenment. Because once we have found our true love, we have reunited with our counterpart—our soulmate. And therefore, we have begun to remember."*

My chest was burning and felt open wider than it ever had, calling for my heart. When Sappho's rustic chest opened, it gave me all my memories back, down to the morning Leto left me on the beach after we'd made love. She had taken it then. In a way, I guess I had known all along. It was always deep in my head, only able to surface through my dreams. I had suppressed it for far too long.

"I need to find her," I said softly, tears beneath my words.

"Who?" Jaden asked.

In my room, I felt alone although Jaden was sitting in front of me. I knew she was still on Earth. I could feel her. I think that was why my chest was burning. She was still here.

"My soul mate," I said. "I need to find Leto."

Chapter 20

One Stormy Night

Soft wind blew against my windowsill and rain sprinkled through the cracks. My fingers went cold as I flicked through the pages of an old encyclopedia from Gaianus, trying to find anything I could on Leto. There was nothing, though. Not a single thing written in our history. I wondered why.

I took a deep breath and smelled the summer rain's soothing scent. Its crackling sound hit the pavement with a soft urgency. The moonlight was bright like the sun, so I drew the shades, but the moon became angry with me and began to shine even brighter. I grew impatient with it—with everything. My eyes were wide-awake and my body restless. Finally, I grabbed my jacket and stepped out into the night.

I followed the curves of the road without caring where they were taking me. The road was sure of its direction, and for that I admired it. Drizzling drops splattered onto the pavement, leaping one by one to their ephemeral fate. Would one drop's soul continue its energy as another drop, or form something greater, an energy that could feel—that could love?

My concentration blew away with the breeze as I counted my steps and the drops that landed on my nose.

Where am I going?

I didn't care.

Must I sleep?

There was no time. My mind was searching and my chest yearning. I was on the brink of finding something great, something amazing, but I didn't know where to look; yet my feet kept moving.

I ended up at the park near the university, where I sat on the swing, looking to the stars for answers. Drops of rain were their only replies. Today was my birthday, I remembered, sitting with the rain. Today was different, a special day, the day I was born, or created by Aphrodite—by Apria. I rolled my eyes at the thought. She was a fake to me now, but also a savior.

I was confused about whether I should be thankful that she'd saved Sappho or pissed that she'd lied to me for more than a century about who she really was. I also wondered if I should be angrier about Ricky trying to convince me that Aphrodite had something to do with Leto leaving me.

I wished for the rain to turn into puzzle pieces then, and as they fell, they would drop into place, beautifully fitting into purpose—into understanding.

"Help me understand this," I cried out.

Doubt clouded my mind. If Zeus and Leto loved each other, why had Leto lied to Sappho—to me? And if it were even true, why would Aphrodite bring Leto to Zeus? Did she know Leto's love was a lie, and had therefore tried to protect Sappho?

I sighed. Although Sappho and Leto's time on the island was thousands of years ago, it had happened to me again yesterday. My immortal life as Petra had completely joined with my mortal life as Sappho.

My stomach ached for my family's inexplicable disappearance. What had happened to them? Would I ever find out? My heart and whole world had been completely shattered because of Leto. I had finally felt love's double-edged sword, just as Apria had never wished for me. I let out a deep and crushing sigh.

My chest was aching still with the slow burn inside. I could feel her out there, somewhere, feel her heart still beating in this world. And if she was out there, I just had to know if she'd ever loved me.

I finally gave the deepest sigh. Was she still with him?

"Why did she love Zeus and not me?" I mumbled aloud.

I looked up, and sprinkles dropped onto my eyelashes. No puzzle pieces.

"Petra?" a soft voice called out from behind me. I turned on the swing and saw Troy on the sidewalk. He was wearing gym clothes and had headphones around his neck.

"What are you doing out here by yourself," he asked, coming closer.

"Why are you jogging this late?" I asked back.

He shrugged and sat down on the swing next to mine. "I couldn't sleep."

"Me either," I mumbled.

He felt agitated, peeved. "I haven't heard from you since you snuck out the other night," he said.

That must be why he's mad.

"I'm sorry," I said candidly.

The breeze sifted through the trees like sand. Chills flowed over my body like shattered glass tearing through my skin. More and more the wind spun the dust off the ground. Suddenly thunder came through the clouds with an Earth-shattering crack, filling the sky with its monstrous voice. The sky developed veins as lightning strikes broke across the darkness.

I looked over at Troy, whose sour expression turned ominous.

"What is it that you want, Petra?" he asked, softly.

I could barely hear him over the thunder, but I didn't need to hear his words to know what he was feeling.

Why does he feel so hurt, so betrayed? All because I left him the other night?

I didn't have a response to give him, and I couldn't decide if he even needed or deserved one. We weren't friends. I barely knew him and really didn't even trust him. I kept looking at him until his face gave up searching for my answer. And for that moment, neither of our minds could read what the other was thinking. We were both blocked—disconnected. I could feel this made him angry.

Thunder cracked again, louder this time, giving me a great start.

"I don't know what else I need to do, Petra!" he yelled over the storm.

I drew my eyes away from the sky to look at him. I saw a God, one of the strongest Gods I knew, in front of me, nearly begging for my heart, and I couldn't find any words to say to him.

Finally, I stood up from the swing and carried my body to his. I put my hands on either side of his swing's chains and stared down at him for the longest time. He looked up at me and stared right back, allowing me in. I slowly leaned down and kissed his brow.

"Then let go," I whispered.

I turned around, took in a deep breath, and began walking where I felt my chest was leading me, toward the mountains and into the woods.

∞

Suddenly, a force greater than gravity began directing my steps. The possibility of greatness had overcome my fear of failure—I was going to find her. There was nothing left to do, and nothing left to say.

Something stronger was inside me: purpose. Like a storm hiding the beauty of the stars, I watched it grow inside me. I felt the roaring thunder rise and the lightning strike harder. Everything was stronger in me.

I wanted to find her. My body was yearning. I needed to find her. My chest burned. I wanted to love her still, and I wanted her to love me. My body needed her love. Why had she betrayed me?

"Why?" I spat at the apathetic mountain. "Did you really not love me?" I cried to the critical moon.

I climbed higher, choking on those words. I was higher than the city, but I wanted to be higher still. The mountain allowed it. I was as great and strong as the mountain. It was my equal, a part of me. I was of the same energy that created it, repeatedly, over millions of years. It was my brother, and I its sister.

Higher I went, digging my toes into my brother's back and my fingers into its chest. I had no light guiding me; the tall trees hid the stormy sky. Instead, my chest was my guide. I didn't question it. I'd broken to the point of insanity.

I reached the top, so high that I could touch the crying Heavens with my fingertips. The skies filled with lightning strikes, which hit the city below. I turned in a slow circle to take in everything around me until my feet finally stopped. Twenty feet from me stood a massive boulder, and someone was sitting on top of it looking down toward the city below.

My stomach dropped to my toes. Slowly, I stepped toward the boulder, my feet sinking into the muddy Earth. I couldn't see their face, but I knew exactly who it was. As I took each step closer, it felt as if the storm slowly began to subside. No more clouds in my chest. There was only a bright blue sky, a beach, an ocean. And so I smiled.

They spun their body around toward me, and my body went motionless as they hopped off the boulder and cautiously made their way to me. The lightning flashed and gave me the courtesy of seeing them. When that happened, I couldn't breathe. It had been her all along. I took many breaths, but still had no air in my lungs. Lightning flashed across the sky again, and this time all I could see were her piercing eyes, those eyes that drew colors from a perfect sea.

Then it came to me as heavy as a wave, as quick as a spark, and as deep as my soul.

I saw her across the school courtyard. As she turned to face me, time slowed down. The sounds and smells around us began to amplify. Her delicate steps so far away, yet so clear. I could hear, without any effort, the soft whispers of the nearby students, who paid no attention to us, for they did not know the importance of what this encounter held.

The hands on the clock began to rewind to the time before our eyes met, before she turned around, before she walked past me. Then the hands slowly came to a stop and then started forward again, to the moment right before she ran into me. Her steps sounded so close. She bumped into me and time stopped. Every face around us froze in place. Life and everything we knew came to a standstill. Her scent was so sharp, a scent I would never forget.

Time restarted. She ran into me, knocking all my papers to the ground. She started to pick them up. I knelt down too, and our eyes locked. Everything began to change—the color of her eyes as brilliant as the sea, her lips a luscious sunset pink, her hair as golden as the sun, and every other color around her saturated to its full potential.

I had never seen anything more beautiful, and it was not just her physique, but the beauty in her eyes. Life's video paused once again, and for that moment Chronos blessed me with more time than I deserved. I stared at her longer than any mortal could have, completely absorbed. What had I done to earn this blessing from the Gods? What had I done to earn this time, this precious time?

Her eyes were all mine in that moment. As beautiful and perfect as they were, I loved them not only for that, but also for the feeling of familiarity that fell over my soul. The Gods had granted me more than just time; they had granted me a memory. A memory that had been stowed away—one I never knew had been hidden. I had seen these eyes before, and I had felt what they did to me.

I saw us lying in the sand a thousand years ago, the moon casting its light on her beautiful face, and for the first time, I saw my soul mate unveiled in front of me. Love had kissed me, giving me her power to awaken my heart and therefore my soul. I could finally breathe. I was finally alive.

The hands on the clock sped up, too fast to see what moment it was landing on next. Faster and faster time pushed forward—days passed, months, years, decades, and centuries. Faster and faster, and then finally, my mind woke up with a gruesome burn in my chest.

I was back in the present time standing in front of her. Crashing thunder and soaring lightning in the sky behind us. She walked closer to me, and just then lightning hit, lighting up her face so I could see her once again. Her face and body were different from her past self, but her eyes were just the same.

My lips could barely form her name, but from my chest I felt it come out on a breath, "Taylor?"

Made in the USA
Monee, IL
27 May 2021

69647167R10100